Curious Magic

Also by
ELISABETH BERESFORD

Awkward Magic
Dangerous Magic
Invisible Magic
Travelling Magic

Curious Magic

ELISABETH BERESFORD

ELSEVIER/NELSON BOOKS
New York

Library of Congress Cataloging in Publication Data

Beresford, Elisabeth.
Curious magic.

SUMMARY: A boy's vacation on an island off the
coast of England brings him in contact with a
white witch, a girl his own age with increasing
magic powers, a boy from the sea, and travel
backwards in time.
[1. Magic—Fiction.   2. Space and time]
I. Title.
PZ7.B4486Cu 1980   [Fic]   80-14916
ISBN 0-525-66682-6

Published in the United States by Elsevier/Nelson Books,
a division of Elsevier-Dutton Publishing Company, Inc.,
New York.

Printed in the U.S.A.   First U.S. Edition

10   9   8   7   6   5   4   3   2   1

Contents

To Kate Waterfall—
Who knows the island well

CHAPTER I

The Island

IT'S NOT EVERYBODY who is lucky enough to be asked to spend his winter vacation on an island. Andy Jones's mother kept telling him this, and although in his heart of hearts he agreed with her, being Andy he had to argue about it.

"It would have been much better if I could've gone in the summer," he said. "In the summer I could've swam."

"Swum," said Mrs. Jones, pushing him off the kitchen table so that she could lay the table for supper, "and I think you're very lucky to have been asked at all. It's very kind of Mr. and Mrs. Dunk to have thought of asking you. We could do with a bit of luck when all's said and done," she said, with a small sigh.

Both of them looked up at the ceiling and its big, damp patch that seemed to get larger every day. The "Horrible Landlord," as they called him, never did anything about repairs, and only last week had had the nerve to write and say that the rent might be going up soon.

"What's the island like, Mum?" Andy asked quietly. He hated seeing his mother's mouth turning down at the corners. Usually she was quite a cheerful person, but recently she had started sighing to herself and frowning when she thought Andy wasn't looking.

"I can hardly remember. Get the bread out. I was only small at the time I went there, much younger that you are now. It's a lovely place. It's got a special feeling about it. There seemed to be miles and miles of sandy beaches and some big cliffs, and there were cows everywhere. I was scared half to death of them, never having seen a real-live cow before, and they weren't shut in behind fences or anything. Just tied to posts with bits of old rope, they were. I always thought that rope looked none too safe. Wash your hands. . . ."

"What else?" asked Andy, giving his hands a quick rinse, which turned them from dark gray to pale gray.

"Use the soap. It's not just for looking at. What else? Oh, yes, we sailed over in a nice little boat. Well, I thought it was nice until the sea got a little rough and then, dear me, it was quite another story. Still, you're lucky, you're going on a plane. *That'll* be exciting. It's not everybody that's lucky enough . . ."

Mrs. Jones should have touched wood and whistled at that point, because the very next evening Andy was quite sure that he saw a burglar climbing into the superintendent's shed. So naturally he went to have a look, missed his footing in the half-light and had an extremely nasty fall. There was a horrible pain in his ankle and then Andy distinctly heard something go "click".

An hour later, still very green around the mouth and with a great deal of heavy white plaster from his toes to his knee, Andy hobbled painfully out of the hospital with his arm around his mother's neck. The "burglar" had turned out to be the super's big black cat, which had since taken fright at all the commotion and vanished into the night.

"Serves you right," the super said crossly, "goodness knows where my Black Bess has got to. Run over, like as not. I'll hold you to blame if she has been, young man, make no mistake about it. Too inquisitive by half, you are. And just look at the damage you've done to my shed! I will write to the landlord. . . ."

Neither Andy nor his mother felt like arguing (for once), and it was a decidedly depressed twosome who faced each other across the kitchen table.

"Well, that's that, then," said Andy's mother, "you can say good-bye to your vacation on the island, that's certain."

"No, it isn't. . . ."

"Yes, it is. You can't go over to the island all done up in a plaster cast to stay with Mr. and Mrs. Dunk at the Fort. You'd never manage."

"Oh, yes, I would," said Andy, who, in spite of his leg hurting quite badly, was just starting to feel like arguing again. "I'd manage okay. I got up the stairs to the apartment all right. And I won't have to go climbing any cliffs or anything. I'll just do some *gentle* sort of exploring. And eating," he added hopefully. He had stopped feeling sick and his stomach was starting to remind him that it was long past suppertime.

"Oh, you," said his mother, giving him an affectionate cuff around the ears, "you're always hungry. It'll have to be eggs and sausages."

"And home fries?"

"You *are* feeling better. But all the same," said Mrs. Jones, reaching for the frying pan, "all the same, young man, I'll have to ask the supervisor at work tomorrow if I can use the telephone and call Mrs. Dunk. She may not fancy having a wounded soldier on her hands. I daresay she's got enough on them already with that big place to look after. You *would* have to go and do something like this when your plane's all booked and everything. Awkward you are. Always pushing your nose into things that don't concern you. Like the time you rescued that 'lost' dog and we had its owner around here saying you'd kidnapped it and . . . Andy, are you all right?"

"What?"

Andy shook his head. He hadn't been listening to what his mother had been saying for the last couple of minutes, since he had heard it all many times before. Anyway, he liked finding out things and it wasn't really poking his nose into other people's business, it was more like just keeping his eyes open for anything interesting that might be going on. And while all this was going through his mind he had quite distinctly heard something. It wasn't the TV of the people in the apartment next door, or the traffic out on the street, because they were sounds he knew very well. It was something quite different, a sort of slapping sound like water slopping around in a bath and beyond that a voice muttering. Only the voice was so faint he couldn't make out the words.

"What?" Andy repeated. "Yes, I'm fine. I guess it's the injection thing that made me... Can I have a *double* portion of potatoes, Mum?"

During the next three days Mrs. Jones tried over and over again to call up Mrs. Dunk on the island to explain about Andy and his leg. Each time the operator told her kindly but firmly that the telephone at the Fort was out of order. On the last occasion the operator, who had heard all about Andy and the vacation and the leg several times over, said, "I'm very sorry, dear, but there's still trouble on the line. It's been reported to the supervisor and—this is strictly confidential, mind—the supervisor says they're always having trouble on that particular number. It's been tested and retested over and over and it's fine for a bit and then it breaks down again. Very strange. Perhaps the salt water gets to it or something. Sorry, dear."

"Well, that's that, then," said Andy's mother with another sigh. "Mr. and Mrs. Dunk'll have to take you as you are, plaster and all. How is it?"

"It tickles," said Andy. "it tickles like anything, but it doesn't hurt exactly."

"Andy, promise me one thing," said Mrs. Jones, looking up from the suitcase she was packing.

"What?" Andy asked cautiously.

"That you won't go sticking your nose into everything... that you'll behave *properly*. Curiosity killed the cat, you know!"

"I'll be as good as gold," said Andy, crossing his fingers behind his back. "Can I have that knitting needle for scratching inside the cast? I wonder if I'll be able to sit behind the pilot on the plane?"

It was a very small bright yellow plane with three engines, one each on the wings and one on the tail. The crew consisted of one person, the pilot. Andy managed to have a few words with him (some people might have called it an argument) and it ended with the pilot's saying extremely firmly, "One more word out of you, young man, and you'll have the seat right at the back with the luggage. And there isn't even a window there, so you won't be able to see anything at all! Now hop it, if you *can* hop, that is."

Andy hopped.

It was only a short flight, but Andy had been a bit worried that he might get overcome by pangs of hunger just the same, so he had spent some of his vacation money at the airport restaurant on a hamburger and Coke. Five minutes after takeoff he wished he hadn't and five minutes after that he had forgotten all about the ache and itch in his leg and was wishing very much indeed that he hadn't eaten anything at all for at least the last twelve hours. There was a strong tail wind and a great deal of wispy gray cloud and the plane seemed to be jumping around quite a bit.

"Umsph!" said Andy, closing his eyes.

When he opened them again the cloud had vanished and he could see a large expanse of gray ocean topped with little ruffles of white foam and beyond that a murky gray shape. The sound of the engines changed and Andy suddenly felt as if two hands were being pressed against his ears and then he could hardly hear anything at all. At the same moment the hamburger and the Coke chose to rise up very sharply from his stomach to the bottom of his throat.

"Er-umsph," said Andy, and he lost interest in the island and everything else until there was a thump-thump-thump and all the muffled noise vanished.

Very slowly Andy opened one eye and then the other. Then he swallowed deeply, and miraculously his airport snack sank back into its proper place in his stomach. The only parts of him that didn't seem to be working were his ears: They continued to feel as if they were stuffed with cotton.

The little plane taxied to a halt and a couple of minutes later Andy found himself thumping into the airport building, which was about the size of the soccer field at school. There were quite a number of people milling about, so Andy just stood still, feeling rather lost and not particularly well, until a man, not much taller than Andy and with a large nose and very bright blue eyes, came up to him and said: "You'll be Andy Jones then, eh? Welcome to the island. I'm Mr. Dunk from the Fort. What *have* you done to yourself? You're a real wounded soldier, you are. Hee-haw, hee-haw. Come along, come along. The van's outside. A rough ride, was it? Well, you're here now and safe and sound and very lucky to be spending your vacation on the island. You look a bit green. You're probably rather deaf, just blow your nose and you'll be all right. That'll get rid of the deafness, eh?"

Andy did as he was told and suddenly there was a click-click in his ears and he could hear properly.

"It wasn't really a bad flight..." Andy began, but he

spoke to the empty air, for Mr. Dunk had already gone outside and was now hurrying off toward the parking lot. Andy picked up his suitcase with some difficulty and followed his host. He wasn't at all sure that he was going to enjoy this vacation in spite of all his mother had said, and he felt a touch of homesickness for the apartment. Even the damp patch and the Horrible Landlord didn't seem too bad for a moment.

"Come on, come on," shouted Mr. Dunk, climbing into a battered white van, "we can't keep Mrs. Dunk waiting. She was saying only this morning that it's not every boy who is . . ."

"Lucky enough to spend his vacation on an island," muttered Andy, and he climbed up awkwardly into the van and sat down with a sigh of relief as he stretched out his bad leg.

CHAPTER II

The Fort

THE FORT turned out to be a letdown, since Andy had expected to find a castle with turrets and a drawbridge. Instead, after a very bumpy ride over cobbled roads, Mr. Dunk suddenly swerved to the right down a sandy lane, drove into a dune, and stopped in front of a dumpy, gray stone building.

"Home," announced Mr. Dunk triumphantly.

Since he had driven the entire two miles in the middle of the road, very fast in second gear and completely ignoring any other traffic, he really had something to feel quite triumphant about.

"Is this it?" asked Andy, who felt as if every tooth in his head had been rattled loose during the hair-raising jour-

ney. But Mr. Dunk had already gone hurrying off under a
stone archway. Andy climbed down, hauled his case after
him, and looked at the Fort.

It was certainly a very solid building, with its high gray
walls and low-pitched roof. There was a kind of central
courtyard beyond the arch, which once upon a time might
have been quite attractive, but now grass and brambles
grew all over it, climbing up hillocky banks to the left until
they reached the top of a high stone wall. There were a
great many little outbuildings, all joined by crumbling
stairs and paths, and Andy saw at once that, if it hadn't been
for his bad leg, there were a lot of places he would have
liked to have explored. It was as if one part of the Fort were
still a place in which people could live quite comfortably,
while the other half had crumbled away. There was also a
distant sighing sound, which came and went regularly, and
for a moment Andy couldn't think what it could be until a
sea gull floated overhead going "Ah-ah-AH," and then he
realized that on the other side of that high wall was the sea.

"Come on, soldier," said Mr. Dunk, suddenly appearing
out of a doorway on the right, "here's Mrs. Dunk waiting to
see you and it's suppertime. It's pot pie with apple crumble
and island cream to follow."

Andy's spirits, which had been rather low, revived.

The kitchen had a wooden floor, a big table, chairs,
shelves, and a large warm stove. Mrs. Dunk was smaller
than Andy and she had bright-blue eyes that went up at the
corners, gray hair, pink cheeks, and a very soft, high voice.
She made Andy think of a field mouse he had once found on
the school soccer field.

"So glad you're," she said and stopped.

"Glad you're here," translated Mr. Dunk, who was already sitting at the table with his knife and fork grasped in his hands, although there was no food on the table yet. "He's a real wounded soldier, he is. How did you do it, eh? Playing soccer? Skateboarding? Falling off a ladder? Hee-haw, hee-haw, hee-haw."

"I was chasing a burglar. At least I *thought* it was a burglar, only it wasn't, it was a cat. Mum did try and telephone you, only . . ."

"Telephone's been out of order for days," said Mr. Dunk, turning around and looking over his shoulder at his wife, who was dishing up the meal, which smelled delicious. "So has the TV and the radio. Only last week we had trouble with the heater too. It's the island. Things are always going wrong here. Mrs. Dunk's fed up with it. She wants to get back to the mainland and I can't say I blame her."

"It is very annoying," said Mrs. Dunk, putting a large helping of pie in front of Andy. "Eat up, now. Is your leg very?"

"Painful?" Said Mr. Dunk, helping himself to Worcestershire sauce so energetically that some of it flew across the table.

"It itches, rather than hurts," said Andy. "Mum lent me a knitting needle to scratch with. Is the Fort very old?"

"Roman," said Mr. Dunk with his mouth full, so that it came out as "Froman." "At least, the oldest part is, like that wall there. It's almost three feet thick in parts. Then it was added on to here and there. We're at the very end of the island, and they do say—I'd like a second helping, please—that the bay was the old harbor hundreds of years ago. And a slice of bread. Thanks. I can't see it myself because it's a very shallow bay, but then I daresay they had very small boats in those days. Then there were the smugglers and pirates, who they *say* used to come ashore here. . . ."

"Smugglers and pirates?" asked Andy, his eyes shining. With Mrs. Dunk's pie inside him he was feeling better and better by the minute. He had even forgotten the itch underneath his cast.

"You don't want to listen to those nasty stories," said Mrs. Dunk. "Have some apple?"

"Crumble," said Mr. Dunk. "Thanks very much. Well, how's your mother?"

Andy, between mouthfuls of the dessert said that his mother was very well, and that she liked working in a cafeteria although she did get a bit sick of always cooking such enormous quantities of food every day.

"There," said Mrs. Dunk, giving Andy a second helping of crumble and a big dollop of cream, "your mother always was a wonderful."

"Cook," agreed Mr. Dunk, "just like Mrs. Dunk here. They were in the same cooking class together at school, you know. That's how they met in the first place. That's how we met too. It was over cheese omelet when Mrs. Dunk was working there in a café. Only, of course, she wasn't Mrs. Dunk *then*! Is there any cheese? All that driving's made me hungry."

It seemed hours later that Andy was taken up a wooden staircase to his bedroom. What with one thing and another, he felt so tired that he hardly had the strength to brush his teeth.

"You'll be all right?" asked Mrs. Dunk, hovering in the doorway. "I won't call you in the."

"Morning," agreed Andy. "What's that flashing over there?"

"It's the mainland lighthouse. Three long flashes and then two short. I hope it won't bother."

Mrs. Dunk nodded and smiled and then tiptoed away. Andy leaned his elbows on the very broad windowsill, pushed his bad leg into a comfortable position, and gazed out over the sea. His bedroom was high enough for him to be able to look over the big seawall, and before him stretched a long, curving sandy bay that glistened like silver in the winter moonlight. Here and there were black patches, which he guessed were rocks and pools, and to the right was the outgoing sea. It was a misty gray, with a thin ripple of moonlight like a narrow, shifting path dappling across it. Andy had never seen anything like it before, and he couldn't help staring and staring at it in a dreamy, tired kind of way. And then, just for a moment, he saw—or thought he saw—a very small shadow moving against the tide, so that it was coming in to shore while the sea was moving out.

Andy narrowed his eyes and looked as hard as he could. Then he saw another small dark figure go running along the silver-colored sand to meet the incoming shadowy shape. The two of them came together at the water's edge. They appeared to be talking, so Andy leaned forward, although he knew he was too far away to hear a word. It was all very strange and interesting and, being Andy, he was extremely curious about what could be going on.

"Bed?" said a voice from the doorway. "Come on, wounded soldier. Into bed with you."

"But . . ." said Andy, and then he suddenly felt too tired to argue. He hobbled across to his bed and climbed into it. Tomorrow he would gently explore parts of the Fort and have a look at the bay and try to work out what he had seen.

"Good night, Mr. Dunk."

"Good night and sleep tight, soldier."

The door of Andy's bedroom was banged shut and Mr. Dunk went clattering down the wooden staircase. At the same time Andy could hear the soft sighing of the waves, the distant call of a seabird, and then, mixed in with all these pleasant sounds, he seemed to hear that faint voice that had echoed inside his head just after he had left the hospital. Only now he could *just* hear what the voice was saying.

"Fish, skin, and tails, the dratted thing's playing up again. Hold steady, do. There, that's more like it, my flower. Here we go then. Rescue. Rescue. Rescue. Res . . ."

The voiced faded away completely.

"Rescue *who* from *what*?" Andy asked the darkness. "I'll have to find out tomorrow. . . ."

And he rolled over and in spite of the bad leg was asleep in two minutes flat.

CHAPTER III

Ella and the
Green Boy

IT SEEMED NO TIME AT ALL until he was awakened by a tremendous crash and the sound of someone shouting.

"Pirates!" he said, shooting up in bed. "There's been a wreck . . . a ship's gone aground . . . it's smugglers."

He forgot about his leg and tried to leap to his feet, with the result that he and all the top bedclothes found themselves on the wooden floor. Andy frantically burrowed his way free and then stopped short as he saw two legs waving backward and forward in front of his window which, fortunately, was open at the bottom. The legs swung over his windowsill, followed by the rest of Mr. Dunk. He was covered in dust and plaster, and he looked quite upset as he sat down heavily on the end of Andy's bed, making all the springs go "wooooing."

"Nasty," said Mr. Dunk, "very nasty," as he slapped at his clothes, sending little clouds of dust in all directions. "Always sleep on the floor, do you?"

"No. I . . ."

"Suit yourself, of course, it's entirely up to you. There was Mrs. Dunk saying she wouldn't be without a TV for another evening, so just to oblige I got up on the ladder and climbed onto the roof to have a look at the aerial, which was lying flatter than you are now, and what happens?"

"You . . ."

"That's right. One of the slates comes clean away and there's me slipping and sliding like a sand eel till I gets to the guttering. And there I hangs until that breaks, too. Not all of it, mind, just a bit, and the next thing I know I'm coming through your window—lucky it was open. I never knew such a place. It's falling to bits all right and no mistake. Well, breakfast time and it's fish by the smell. Better get a move on. Mrs. Dunk doesn't like to be kept waiting."

Mr. Dunk got up, making the bed springs go "woooing" again, and stumped over to the door, which he shut behind him with a bang. A solitary slate slid past the window and there was a distant crash, followed by a yelping noise. By the time Andy managed to go and look out, there was nothing to see but a lot of broken guttering and slates lying in the sandy brambles.

Breakfast, which was porridge, kippers, toast and honey, made Andy feel strong enough to go off and do some exploring. He wanted to try and track down the mysterious voice he had heard, or thought he had heard, the night before. He decided to ask a few tactful questions.

"Does anybody else live around here?" he asked.

"There's Tommy," said Mrs. Dunk, "you didn't meet him last night. He's shy of."

"Strangers," agreed Mr. Dunk. "I'll have another slice of toast. Thanks. He's our dog. Lovely dog he is, too. A German pointer. Very highly bred and nervous in his ways. Mind you, he's very gentle and once he gets to know you he's most affectionate. Come to think of it, he might like you to take him for a walk. I would, of course, only I've got a lot to do. Sweeping up."

"Are there any people?" asked Andy.

"Oh, *people*," said Mr. Dunk. "During the summer, there are any number of people living hereabouts. The Fort's full of them. There are two self-contained apartments here, you know. But during the winter there's just Mrs. Tressida. A dear old lady she is, but keeps herself to herself. Got a young relation staying with her at the moment. Funny little creature. Up and down the bay all day, shrimping and that. But she never seems to catch much. Well, it stands to reason she won't at this time of year. I think shrimps are like tortoises, they go to sleep when it's cold and . . ."

"*Where* do they live?" asked Andy, who was just starting to learn that the only way to stop Mr. Dunk when he was talking was to talk himself.

"The shrimps? In the rock pools. Big, fat, fine shrimps you get in the summer. Now in the winter . . ."

"Mrs. Tressida and the little girl are in the flat next to," said Mrs. Dunk.

"Me?" said Andy. "Oh, great, that could be what I heard last night."

"They don't have a TV," said Mr. Dunk, getting up and going to sit beside the stove. "Do you know, I'm really tired out. Perhaps I'll sweep up a little bit later on. No, you couldn't have heard *them* talking, not through these walls. Mrs. Dunk'll get Tommy for you and then you can take him for a walk. He'll enjoy that."

Andy wasn't at all sure that *he'd* like it much, since he didn't know a lot about dogs; but Tommy turned out to be just as uneasy about Andy as Andy was about him. He was a very beautiful white- and liver-colored animal with melting brown eyes. He whined and shivered a little, sniffing at the plaster cast, and then he suddenly seemed to make up his mind that Andy wasn't an enemy but a friend, and he put his front paws on Andy's shoulders and licked his ears.

"There," said Mr. Dunk, who was gently dozing off in front of the stove, "didn't I tell you that he'd be pleased to take a walk with you? Mrs. Dunk'll give you his leash, but you can let him off it when you're on the beach. Just give a whistle and he'll come back to you when you want him. My word, I *am* tired. It's all that work."

Andy would have much rather explored the rest of the Fort and perhaps called on his mysterious neighbors, but somehow he and Tommy found themselves bustled outside and onto the long, curving sandy beach. Andy soon discovered that it was quite difficult walking on sand with his bad leg, especially since Tommy kept trying to get away, so the easiest thing was to undo the leash. Tommy shook himself, gave Andy a "please-excuse-me" look, and bolted. He ran quite beautifully, like a racehorse, and in no time at all he had vanished over the distant rocks.

"Oh! Come back! Here, boy! TOMMY!" yelled Andy.

He put his fingers in his mouth and whistled piercingly.

But Tommy stayed invisible and Andy heaved a deep sigh and began plodding across the sand after him. There was quite a stiff breeze and the sea was scudding sideways across the bay and throwing itself onto the shore, sending up little clouds of spray.

Andy blundered on until he reached a huddle of sharp-looking rocks. Since he was feeling out of breath and his leg was hurting a bit, he decided to take a rest, so he sat down. Apart from anything else, he wanted to have a little time to think over all that had happened since he had arrived on the island. For one thing, there had been those two dark shadows he had seen last night. It could have been, perhaps, two smugglers meeting each other. And then there had been that faint voice that had said, "Rescue, rescue, rescue. . . ." although who wanted to be rescued and from what he hadn't the faintest idea.

It was at that exact moment that Andy, with his back against the cold, hard rocks in the middle of an apparently empty beach, became aware that he was not alone at all, because just over his shoulders he heard someone say, "I thought you said she could help me!"

"Yes, well, I expect she will be able to. Only everything keeps going wrong at the moment. Everything!"

"Yes, well, I'm sorry. But what about me? It's not much fun being the odd one out. The others all keep laughing at me. I can't help it if I'm different. It's only because it's high tide again that I've been able to get away. They'll be looking for me soon."

"Oh dear, oh dear," the second voice said distractedly, "I don't know what to do and . . . oh, what's that?"

"It's a dog and it's coming this way. Quick, give me a hand."

There was a grunting noise as if somebody were trying to lift something heavy, and at the same time the sound of barking grew nearer and nearer.

Andy, who had been listening with enormous interest to this conversation, although it had nothing to do with him, balanced himself on his good leg and somehow managed to scramble up the sharp rocks so that he could look over the top. Below him was a narrow gully of sand with high rocks on three sides of it. The fourth side was open to the sea and covered in thick, brown, slippery seaweed.

Kneeling on the sand, with her back to Andy, was a girl whose long fair hair was being blown back and forth in the sharp winter breeze. Beyond her Andy could see the head and shoulders of a boy with a very pale green face. He was half lying down, supporting himself on his hands, and his bright emerald eyes noticed Andy at once.

"Somebody here," he said breathlessly.

The girl turned around and looked up. Her pointed little face was wearing an extremely worried expression. So worried, in fact, that for one awful moment Andy thought she might start crying.

"It's only me, you know," he said quickly. "I mean I'm Andy Jones and I'm staying at the Fort just along the beach. And I think the dog is probably Tommy. He's from the Fort, too. He won't hurt you. He's a very gentle sort of dog, really."

"I'm not afraid of dogs," the boy said fiercely, "but—" And then he stopped suddenly in much the same way that Mrs. Dunk did.

"I only meant . . ."

"Oh, never mind," interrupted the girl. "The trouble is that dogs don't like . . . don't like Mervyn. Please get hold of Tommy and hang on to him."

"I'll do my best," Andy said doubtfully, "but I think I'd better tell you that . . ."

"Oh, go *on*. Hurry!" the girl said, flapping her hands at him.

Andy slid rather painfully down the rock to do his best. Even with two good legs he knew he hadn't the faintest chance of catching Tommy. With one bad leg it would be an impossible task. Still, the situation seemed to be pretty desperate, so he hobbled around the rocks and onto the soft sand just as Tommy came careering toward him with his ears back, his eyes rolling, and all his teeth and gums showing in a very frightening way. He looked extremely fierce and not at all like the shy, nervous animal who had given him a friendly lick earlier. Now he was more like a wolf chasing its prey.

However, there just wasn't any time in which to be scared, and somehow Andy managed to heave himself around the rocks so that he was between them and Tommy.

"TOMMY!" Andy bellowed so loudly that a whole flock of gulls took to the air in fright.

Tommy checked for a split second, his paws scudding on the soft sand so that he made four long furrows. He shook his head from side to side, showing the whites of his eyes, and then with a deep snarl he jumped for the rocks. Andy had a brief glimpse of a tawny brown-and-white body going over his head and he clutched at it, with the result that he went over backward with a thump that almost winded him, but he managed to hang on, linking his fingers together behind Tommy's back.

The two of them rolled over and over, with Tommy heaving and pulling to get free and snarling horribly while Andy, with equal determination and with his eyes, nose, mouth, and ears full of sand, hung on. It was like being the second dog in a dog fight. And then, quite suddenly, when Andy knew he couldn't hold on any longer because he couldn't breathe, Tommy went quite limp and collapsed in a heavy, shivering heap. With very shaky fingers Andy clipped the leash onto Tommy's collar and dropped the loop of the leash over a strong finger of rock. Then he rolled over onto his face to try to get his breath back.

"Are you dead?" asked an anxious voice from a long way away.

"I'm not sure," Andy muttered.

He felt sick and giddy and quite a few bits of him, apart from his leg, were hurting pretty badly. Cautiously he opened his eyes and saw that the girl was sitting beside him with her hands clasped around her hunched knees.

"I'm sorry about your leg," she said. "I didn't know about it."

"Well, it helped in a way, because it made me heavier. Did Mervyn escape?"

"Mervyn? Oh, yes, *Mervyn*. Yes, he did, thank you. And thank you for rescuing him."

She hesitated as though trying to make up her mind about something and, although Andy was longing to ask dozens of questions, he actually managed to keep quiet, because he had a feeling that the girl was going to tell him

something important. When she did speak it was a bit of a
letdown.

"I think you'd better meet my—great-aunt, Mrs. Tressida," she said; "come on."

It wasn't until they were halfway across the beach with a
very docile Tommy shivering at their heels, that Andy
realized that there was no third set of footprints leading
from the rocks.

Mervyn had gotten away all right. By using the same
route by which he had arrived on the beach last night—by
swimming.

CHAPTER IV

The White Witch

THE GIRL led the way under the stone arch of the Fort and then past the main part of the building where the Dunks lived. Through the kitchen window Andy caught a glimpse of Mrs. Dunk washing dishes and Mr. Dunk fast asleep in front of the stove.

"This way," the girl said briskly. She turned a corner at the back of the Fort, and Andy saw for the first time that between the main building and the high seawall there was a curving stone stairway. Bits of it were missing and some of the steps were overgrown with weeds and grass. They were all so steep that Andy would have found it rather hard going if Tommy hadn't dragged him up. He was now being extra friendly and good and helpful, as though he wanted to make up for his earlier bad behavior.

The girl stopped in front of a battered wooden door and gave it a push with her shoulder.

"In here," she said, "but you'd better leave Tommy outside."

Tommy had no intention of being left anywhere, and he wound himself in and out of Andy's legs, shivering and whining and looking up with sad, rolling brown eyes.

"Stupid dog," muttered Andy. "Oh, look out. . . ."

The leash and Tommy and the bad leg all seemed to get mixed up together in the narrow passage and Andy found himself hopping backward into a long, low-ceilinged room. When he and Tommy had stopped going around and around and had finally sorted themselves out, Andy was at the far end of the room and face to face with a tiny old woman who was sitting in a very large armchair and looking at him with great interest. She had a lot of white hair all done up in a big bun, a wrinkled little face, round spectacles, and very bright black eyes. Her hands were clasped on the top of a stick and she was wearing a blue dress and fluffy white bedroom slippers.

"Good morning," she said in a soft gentle voice, "you'll be Andrew Jones, staying with Mr. and Mrs. Dunk, I daresay. Sit down, then. Ella, shoo off that cat, do."

An extremely large white cat, which had been hunching its back and sticking up its tail as it gazed at Tommy, leaped into the girl's arms and then hung itself around her neck so that it looked for all the world like a furry white shawl. Tommy gazed up at it and then retreated step by step behind a sofa, until only the end of his brown-and-white tail was showing.

"They've met before," said the old woman. "I'm Mrs.

Tressida, and that's Ella. The cat's name is Lolly, but she'll answer to nearly anything. She's got no sense at all. Well, about the same amount of sense as Tommy there. Go on, ask away."

"It's you!" said Andy, who was bursting with curiosity and questions. "It's your voice that I've been hearing in my head, isn't it?"

"It is indeed. And a fair old time of it I've been having trying to talk to you. It's been worse than the phonetele."

"Telephone," said Ella. "I hope it's all right me bringing Andrew here, but he did rescue . . . well, me, you know. And he's got a bad leg."

"Of course, I know," said Mrs. Tressida sharply. "He's the one we've been waiting for, all right."

"Is he *really*? He doesn't look like I imagined he would."

"Wounded knights come in all shapes and sizes."

"Now look here," said Andy, so loudly that he made himself jump. "Will somebody please explain what's going on? Because I don't understand anything at all."

"Of course you don't," agreed Mrs. Tressida. "How could you? Does your leg hurt much?"

"It sort of aches a bit. Well, quite a lot."

"There's not much I can do to put it right with that nasty great thing on it," said Mrs. Tressida, peering at the plaster cast first through her round spectacles and then over the top of them. "Give me your hands, Andy, and we'll see if that'll help."

Andy rubbed some of the sand off on his duffel coat and held out his hands. Mrs. Tressida put them gently palm to palm and then clasped her tiny, rather rheumaticky hands over his. They were warm and dry and very gentle, and after

a moment or two Andy began to feel almost drowsy and he
found himself blinking and staring at the log fire, where the
flames seemed to be getting blurry. At the same time all the
aches and scratchiness began to melt away, and even the
pain in his ankle started to lessen until it wasn't there at all.

"Better?" asked Mrs. Tressida as Andy let out a gusty
sigh of relief.

"Yes, much. Thanks. But how did you do it?"

"It's like learning to ride a . . . well, learning to ride.
Once you've got the trick of it, you've got it forever. Well,
seeing that it's worked so well with you makes me even
more sure that you're the one who'll rescue me. Won't
you?"

Andy took a very deep breath, folded his arms across his
chest, and stuck out his chin. He hadn't the faintest idea
what Mrs. Tressida was talking about, he had no notion
what was going on and he felt as if his brain were full of
cotton. But one thing he *was* quite sure about was that he
wasn't going to try and rescue anybody from anything until
he discovered exactly what all this was about.

"Would you please explain?" he said, his voice so stern
he hardly recognized it himself. Lolly stopped washing
herself and Tommy edged even farther around the back of
the sofa so that the tip of his tail vanished. Ella hunched her
knees up to her chin and muttered.

"Oh, Aunt Tressida, are you *really* sure?"

"Sure as I'll ever be, my flower. Very well, Andy, I'll
explain right from the beginning, which is a long time ago.
But before I do I'll have to ask *you* one question, and a very
important question it is, too. Ready?"

"Yes."

"It's this then: Do you believe in magic?"

"You mean like conjuring tricks? Sawing people in half and getting rabbits to come out of hats and all that?"

"No, no, no!" Mrs. Tressida thumped her stick up and down. "That's just silly stuff any fool can do with training. I mean *real* magic."

"I don't think I've ever seen any," Andy said cautiously, "and, anyway, magic things happened years and years ago in history. Magic stopped with telephones and radios and TV and the Concorde. It's old-fashioned."

"That's where you're all wrong, my flower. I'll admit that there isn't as *much* magic around as there used to be, but there's still a fair amount of it, only everybody's in such a hurry these days they don't bother to stop and look for it. You don't bother to use your eyes and ears anymore. It's not magic that's getting old-fashioned, it's curiosity. You just sit in front of your visiontele sets . . . "

"Television sets," said Ella.

"That then," agreed Mrs. Tressida. "You never look over your shoulders at the rest of the world. You don't ask questions."

"I do," said Andy. "In fact, Mum says I ask far too many. How do you know so much about magic?"

"That's better," said Mrs. Tressida. "Well, I *should* know, because I've been in magic all my life, and a very long life it's been, too. Magic was my trade, and a proper training we used to have in those days. Will you take my word for it that there's still magic in the world?"

"Well, well . . . there *could* be." Andy said after a long pause. He still wasn't too sure what Mrs. Tressida was talking about as far as all this magic business was concerned, but he did know that he liked getting to the bottom of things and asking questions. "Well, all right, there *could* be."

"Very well, then," said Mrs. Tressida, "it's not much of an answer, but it'll have to do. You *almost* accept magic and it'll *almost* accept you. Now, to begin at the very beginning . . . Is your leg all right still?"

"Yes, thanks. It's even stopped itching."

"Good. Well, once upon a time . . . "

As Mrs. Tressida began to talk Andy found himself looking not at her or Ella, but at the logs in the fireplace, and as the flames went up and down, her voice seemed to keep time with them.

"Once upon a time, a long, long time ago, there was white magic and black magic and a great deal of in-between magic, all going about their business. There were magicians, both good and bad, and it took them years and years to get to the top of their profession, and when they'd taken their final exams they became members of MAT and . . . "

"Mat?" asked Andy.

"Sorry, my flower. That stands for Magic and Allied Trades. Oh, they were proud to get those letters after their names, I can tell you. Out in the desert countries where there's nothing but sand and a few little old palm trees there were the mighty jinns and their assistants, the genies. Always calling up sandstorms they were, or so I've heard. I never had the interest of meeting one of them. Then there was the great phoenix, a wise old bird who had a strange way of laying one egg every hundred years or so and hiding it away, and then he'd build himself a nest and set fire to it and vanish in the flames. And a little while after that the egg would hatch and there'd be the phoenix back again and good as new. It seemed a funny sort of way of going on, but it must have suited his purpose.

"The ones I could never abide personally were the stone creatures. Gargoyles, you call them now, and they're still all over the place. Nasty, squirmy, mischief-making little imps *they* are. It only needs a bit of dark magic to get them on the go, and they're out of their stone as quick as lightning and squealing and fighting all over the place. They're only happy if they can do someone a bad turn. Quite the opposite of the unicorns. Now *they* were lovely creatures. White as fresh snow, but not a brain in their heads, and vain. They were as happy as the day was long if they could just stand admiring their reflections in a pool of water. But they could be brave in times of danger, I'll give them that. I doubt if there's any of them left now, but in those days a troop of unicorns was something to behold.

"And then, of course, there was the mighty Sphinx, which held all the magic secrets of the world in its head, but never told one of them. The Sphinx knew more about magic than all the rest put together, so it was said.

"Those were some, but not all, of the Magic People and creatures that were on the earth, and quite often flying around and about *above* it. And then there were the others. The Sea People. Don't ask me how it came about, for I can't tell you, but it all started to go wrong at the GMCM when . . . "

"GMCM?" asked Andy, who needed a bit of breathing space in which to take in all this extraordinary information.

"Great Magical Council Meeting. They're held every hundred years or so. Anyway it's sufficient to say that the

Sea People, who always were on the difficult side, started picking quarrels with everybody and everything. They all started arguing away—except for the unicorns, who didn't understand what was happening—and finally when it came to the vote, and the mighty Sphinx was in the chair, the Sea People had claimed their right to be in complete control of water. They said, and rightly, I suppose, that three fifths of the world was lakes and oceans and seas, so it should be up to them to govern them.

"The Sphinx did what it could to hold matters together, according to all accounts, but it didn't help, although black, white and in-between land and air magic were all united for once. Which doesn't happen often! But they were out-numbered by the Sea People, and the Sea People got what they wanted: magic control of all waters, worldwide. And from the moment the vote was taken and they'd won—on a show of wings, fins, claws, tails, and so on—that was it. There was land magic and sea magic, and neither side could or would mix with the other. It was a stupid, silly business, and some said that it was all because Old Neap—Young Neap he was called then—who was king of the Sea People, was jealous of the mighty Sphinx. But it was all just talk, I'm sure. But there we were, stuck with it. Well, some were more stuck than others.

"You see, Andy, a few magic Land People found them-selves what you might call trapped. There they were living on little islands and going about their business, such as putting on spells and mixing up potions, but after the vote was taken they had no way of getting back to the mainland. Which was all right for a few hundred years, but then some of them, or maybe just one of them, started to feel what you could call a bit homesick. Homesick for hills and rolling stretches of open countryside and towns and villages, rivers and rooftops. Homesick for the places they knew when they were young . . . "

A log broke in two in the grate and sent up a shower of sparks like a firework display. Lolly unwound herself from Ella's neck and jumped to the floor, sniffed at Andy's plaster cast, and then walked off with her tail sticking straight up. Tommy snored heavily from behind the sofa and Andy blinked, rubbed his eyes, and looked very hard at Mrs. Tressida.

"Hang on," said Andy. "It's a very interesting story, but I remember once, when I was small, reading or hearing something about . . . "

"Go on," said Mrs. Tressida encouragingly, "you're getting there."

"At last," muttered Ella, putting a large black kettle on the logs.

"That . . . " said Andy slowly, "that *witches* can't cross water. Do you mean *you* . . . that you're one of the ones who is stuck because *you* . . . "

Mrs. Tressida's gentle little wrinkled face broke into a smile.

"That's it, my flower," she agreed. "I'm a white witch, and here I am surrounded by water with no chance at all of getting back to the mainland."

"And you," said Ella, sitting back on her heels as the kettle began to send out little puffs of steam, "have been chosen to rescue her."

"Yes, indeed," said Mrs. Tressida. "the Sphinx, who wasn't as yellow as he was sandy-looking, did manage to slip in one saving clause to the agreement. Which was that a white witch could be rescued by a wounded knight. I've been searching for one for many a year and then suddenly clear as night I saw you in the crystal. Well, my flower?"

"Sugar!" said "Sir" Andrew Jones.

CHAPTER V

Two Thousand
Years Ago

"YOU'RE VERY QUIET," said Mr. Dunk at dinnertime.

"Do you feel all right, dear?" asked Mrs. Dunk. "You look quite pale. Is your leg paining?"

"Doesn't hurt a bit, thanks," said Andy truthfully. Most of him was feeling fine, it was just his head that seemed to be going around and around.

"It's all that traveling, I guess," said Mr. Dunk, passing his plate for a third helping. "Mrs. Dunk and me'd like to do some traveling ourselves, but with the high cost of the air fares it's out of the question. I'll have another potato, please. Thanks."

"What we'd really like would be a small place on the mainland," said Mrs. Dunk. "Somewhere where we could have chickens and ducks and grow all our own."

"Vegetables," agreed Mr. Dunk. "There's nothing like homegrown veg. All this responsibility gets me down. Eat up, soldier."

Being called "soldier" sent a shiver right down Andy's back and he nearly dropped his knife.

"Pity about that bad leg of yours," said Mr. Dunk, settling into the chair by the stove, "you could have given me a hand with the TV aerial. I'll just let my dinner go down for a minute or two before I start work."

As Andy helped with washing dishes, Mr. Dunk politely moving his feet out of the way so that Andy could get closer to the sink, it did just cross Andy's extremely muddled mind that Mr. Dunk hadn't actually done any work at all yet, unless one could call falling off the roof work. Mrs. Dunk, on the other hand, never seemed to stop. She was always on the go.

"Thank you, dear," she said as they finished. "What are you going to do this?"

"Afternoon. Going for a walk with Ella."

"So you've met. That's nice. She always looks so worried. Mrs. Tressida's a dear old soul, but they do keep themselves to—"

"And I don't wonder," thought Andy with a muffled snort of laughter as he imagined what Mr. and Mrs. Dunk would say if they knew they had a white witch sharing the Fort with them.

"Aunt's asleep," said Ella, skipping down the stone stairs with a bulging plastic bag over her arm.

"So's Mr. Dunk."

They set off through the arch and across the grassy sand

dunes and up a bumpy track with high blackberry bushes on either side of it. Andy was just starting to pant a bit when Ella turned a corner and apparently vanished straight into the bushes. Andy hurried after her and saw ahead of him a very small square building with a door facing him. Ella gave it a push and beckoned Andy to follow.

"My goodness!" said Andy.

The building was just one room, of which the opposite wall was nearly all window. Since they were now quite high up, there was a wonderful view right over the Fort and across the beach to the distant rocks that Tommy had gone off to explore that morning. The sea was hurrying out now, leaving the sand smooth and clean, except for a dark ripple of seaweed here and there.

"It's an extra guest room for when the Fort's full in the summer," Ella explained. "It's Aunt Tressida's favorite place, because it's got no electric things in it. Electricity and magic can get into an awful mix-up sometimes. At least they do when Aunt's about."

"So *that's* why the TV keeps breaking at the Fort!"

"Yes, it's not her fault. I mean, she doesn't make it happen on purpose."

"And the telephone," Andy said, hoisting himself onto the bunk bed underneath the window. "Mum reported it to the supervisor, because she couldn't get through to Mr. Dunk."

"There are always repair people coming to the Fort," said Ella with a deep sigh. "It makes things ever so difficult. Aunt wanted to go into the shops the other day and the bus broke down halfway up the hill. Which just goes to show why she couldn't possibly get off the island in a plane."

"I should jolly well think *not*," said Andy, going quite pale at the idea. "But, ahem, what about a broomstick? I mean I thought, er, witches used *them* for getting around."

"Aunt gave that up years ago. Ever since her rheumatism started."

"Boat?" suggested Andy. "I mean an ordinary old rowboat sort of boat? Oh . . . "

"Yes," said Ella nodding, "the Sea People would whistle up a storm in five minutes. It's a big problem."

"Is she *really* your aunt?"

"Yes, about nineteen times over my great-aunt. She's enormously old, you know."

"Do you always live with her?"

"You do ask a lot of questions. No, I've just come over for a vacation like you. She's very lonely, I think. Perhaps it's all because of her being homesick. It must be like being away at boarding school for hundreds of years. Now it's my turn to ask. What are you going to do?"

"I haven't got the faintest idea. I don't know anything at all about magic. In fact, I didn't know that there *was* any magic until now. I'm not really a knight, or a wounded soldier or anything, I'm just me. And I live with my mum in a rotten old apartment. I'd like to help Mrs. Tressida, but I don't think I can. In fact I know I can't."

"Aunt says there's no such word as *can't*," replied Ella, pushing back her long hair and reaching into the plastic bag, "and anyway, you've already done some rescuing. I guess it gets quite easy once you get used to doing it. I never thought I could start to learn about magic until I tried. Here we are. I, er, borrowed this from Aunt while she was asleep."

Ella put a small crystal ball on the bunk bed and rolled up her sleeves in a businesslike manner. She put her small hands over the crystal and began to mutter under her breath.

"Here. Hey. I mean, if you're not very good at it . . . "

"Shut up and listen," said Ella fiercely, her face screwed up into the most terrible expression as she concentrated.

Dusk had already started to settle outside, so that the gray winter sea and sky were almost the same color as the sand. Big white clouds were billowing up over the distant mainland and the small, thin-legged oyster catchers were calling to each other at the water's edge. Some pigeons flapped past, and out at sea a much larger bird flew back to its rock, only a wing's span above the cold waves.

It was getting dark inside the little summerhouse, and Andy rubbed his hands across his eyes to make them see better as he stared at the little glass crystal. It was very odd, but it seemed to him that it was starting to glow with a soft green light. Up till that moment he had only really half believed all that Mrs. Tressida and Ella had told him, but suddenly he began to feel a kind of tingling sensation in his fingers and toes and his heart started to go "thump-thump-thump" very loudly. He wanted to say "Hey, what's going on?" but somehow he couldn't speak and all the time the glowing light was getting stronger and stronger and he couldn't look away from it, because it wasn't a small round crystal any longer, but a shifting gray-green mist that was forming into shapes.

"That's you," Andy said huskily.

And certainly a girl who looked similar to Ella was starting to take shape in front of them. It was like watching someone in one of those distorting mirrors at carnivals, or a television set when the controls aren't set properly. And then, with a kind of shake, everything settled down normally and there was Ella's twin gazing back at them with an astonished expression. She had long, rather tangled hair and she was wearing a bunchy sort of gray-green smock and bare feet.

"Here's a surprise and no mistake about it," she said. "Where did you spring from?"

Andy tried to answer, but only a kind of husky "huh huh huh" came out.

"Kitten-cat got your tongue, then?" said the girl. "Here, I know you then, don't I?" And she pointed a rather grubby finger at Ella. Ella only opened and closed her mouth in the manner of a landed fish. The girl giggled and sank back on her heels.

"Well, are you coming over properly, or aren't you?" she asked. "It's no good you hanging around in that mist. Here, give me your hand then. . . . "

And she streatched forward and grabbed hold of the hands of Andy and Ella and jerked them toward her. The first sensible thought that came into Andy's head was that it was suddenly much warmer, quite hot, in fact, and the second was that this was because the sun was directly overhead instead of sinking palely down toward the winter sea, which it had been doing a couple of minutes ago.

"It's summertime," Andy announced very loudly.

"High summer, my flower, and there's no need to shout. I'm not deaf, even if you two seem to be struck dumb."

"I'm not dumb, nor is Ella, and who are you and where are we and why is it summer in the middle of the winter?"

"What a lot of questions. My given name is Tress, you're on the Foreland, and it's always summer in the summertime. Same as it always has been, same as it always will be, I don't doubt. There now, it's vexing. Here's me doing my first proper spell and all I get for my pains and practicing is you two."

Ella knelt down on the bright green grass, took off her duffel coat—it really was a very hot day—and stared hard at her "twin."

"It wasn't you that did the spell, it was me," said Ella.

"No, 'twasn't, 'twas me."

"No, it wasn't."

"Yes, it was."

"No, it . . ."

"Shut up!" roared Andy.

Silence descended between Tress and Ella. They glowered at each other and then at Andy. it really was quite extraordinary looking at the pair of them, because although their clothes were different, their faces were as alike as two peas in a pod.

"First," said Andy, ticking things off on his fingers. "I was with Ella and I saw her talking to the crystal ball. . . ."

"Doing a spell."

"All right, doing a spell. And, secondly, I don't know anything about magic, because we don't learn it in school, although there is chemistry and physics in the upper grades, which I suppose is sort of the same. But it was Ella that did the magic part. So she made us come here. And anyway, I don't know where 'here' is because I've never heard of the Foreland. Ella and I are staying on the island."

"This isn't an island," said Tress. "I don't know what

you're talking about. Any fool knows it's all part of the mainland. And I never heard of any chemistry or physics. I'm a learning white witch and I was doing my homework in between minding the goats. It gets a bit boring being on your own all day, so I thought I'd have a try at magicking up a couple of friends. Then everything went all misty and you two started to appear. You did look funny all rippling like the waves on the sea."

"You looked pretty funny yourself," Ella said coldly.

"Yes, well, don't let's start all that again," Andy put in hurriedly. "Whichever one of you brought us here, what was it *for*? *Why* are we where we are?"

"Well," said Ella, avoiding his eye and rolling up the legs of her jeans, and then kicking off her shoes and socks and lifting up her face to the hot sun, "well, you said you didn't know how to start rescuing Aunt, so I thought I'd see if some magic would help. So *I* said *my* spell and I asked for us to be taken where we *could* help. Only I think, perhaps, I didn't do it quite right."

Ella was starting to get her worried look again, so Andy said quickly, "Well, never mind. Can't be helped. Now we *are* here, we might as well have a look around before we go back."

"There is one thing I've got to tell you," Ella said in a very small voice, her face getting more worried every second. But Andy, always curious about everything, had already moved away.

He felt extremely odd. It wasn't just the upsetting business of moving from one place and time of year to another, it was also because in a weird kind of way Andy felt as if had been to the Foreland before.

The hill behind them was dotted with ferocious-looking goats with great curving horns and long matted coats, and he was thankful to see that they were all tethered. Down below was a smallish stone building with slit windows and a low-pitched roof and a stone archway, through which he could just see a neatly paved forecourt. Surrounding the building were more stone flags that led onto a narrow paved road. There was a cluster of wooden buildings to one side, and through the soft surge of the blue sea and the singing of a skylark Andy could just hear the clatter of hooves, so he guessed that the wooden place was a stable.

Beyond the building was a long, curving sandy beach with several little slipways running down into the sea. At the far end was a wide rocky causeway, which was several miles long and ran straight as a ruler until it reached the distant mainland. It appeared to be quite a busy road, for Andy, straining his eyes through the heat haze, could see several groups of people walking or riding horses along it in both directions.

A small man, wearing a leather tunic and sandals laced up to just below the knees, came hurrying out of the building carrying a very rickety-looking wooden ladder. He glanced up, saw Andy, and called out.

"Hey, there, you boy. Give us a hand, will you? That dratted girl was supposed to be helping me once she'd got the goats tethered, but she's gone mooning off somewhere. What have you done to your leg, then?"

"I . . ."

"Proper wounded soldier, you are. Never mind, it won't stop you from holding the bottom of the ladder. What's the matter? Cat got your tongue?"

"Sorry," mumbled Andy, thumping over the flagstones. Now he knew quite definitely that he was going off his rocker, because the man was familiar, too. He had the same jutting nose and bright blue eyes as Mr. Dunk. Only he wasn't Mr. Dunk at all, but a complete stranger.

"I dunno," the man went on, "they go off on their maneuvers as they call 'em—fun and games I'd call 'em—and leave me with everything to do. It's too much for one man. Look at that roof, now, with half the guttering coming away. Hold it steady, lad. Here, what's your name then?"

Andy told him.

"Funny sort of name. Short for Hadrian, I suppose. Mine's Donkey. Know why? No, of course you don't. It's because they say I laugh like one. Pity about that leg of yours, otherwise you could have gone up the ladder instead of me. I've got no head for heights. Hey, something seems to be happening on the R. Twelve."

"Eh?" said Andy. A very upsetting idea was starting to take shape at the back of his mind, and in spite of the heat of the day a cold, clammy sensation was creeping up his back.

"You *are* ignorant," said Mr. Donkey. "Foreigner, are you, from the other side of the Foreland? Funny lot, you foreigners. No offense meant and none taken, I trust. The R. Twelve is the military road, of course. They say the other end of it goes slap, bang into the middle of Rome itself, but that's all a tale, I daresay. Hey! Look at 'em all running about out there, like a lot of ants. P'raps they've spotted a sea monster. Hee-haw, hee-haw, hee-haw."

And Mr. Donkey put back his head and laughed so loudly that he slid down the ladder, landing with a thump at Andy's feet.

The clammy feeling was getting worse as Andy said hoarsely, "What—what year is this?"

"This year, of course. What other year could it be, soldier? And talking of soldiers," said Mr. Donkey, shading his eyes with his dirty hand, "I don't like the look of this one little bit. See that ship out there? What's it got painted on the side, can you see?"

Andy squinted into the heat haze. Far out on the blue waves he finally spotted a small, odd-looking boat with a high prow and one billowing sail.

"It . . . it looks like a sort of lion with a long tail," he said, "but what *time* is it?"

"High summer, and high time we got a move on," replied Mr. Donkey, who had gone quite pale under his tan. "There, now, wouldn't you know that the moment the garrison is off on its so-called maneuvers the other lot'd get wind of it and come sailing in. It's not right. It's not part of my duty to be responsible for the Fort all on my own. I'll complain, make no mistake about it. Here comes Tress and about time. Got another foreigner with her, too. Well, the more the merrier at the moment. It's all hands to the Treasury . . . "

"Wait," Andy caught desperately at Mr. Donkey's arm. "What is the garrison?"

"You *are* ignorant. The garrison is the Twelfth Roman Legion, of course. That lot out there are raiders from the North Country. Come on, Tress, shift yourself, girl, we've got to get the wages well and truly hidden, and the sooner the better. Now I'll tell you what to do and . . . "

Mr. Donkey's face faded away as far as Andy was concerned, because now he knew for certain what had been hovering at the back of his mind for some time. He and Ella hadn't just moved from winter to summer, they had traveled a great deal farther than that. Quite a few hundred years, in fact, back to when the island wasn't an island at all, but part of the mainland; when the old Fort had been a very new Roman fort. A fort which quite soon was going to be attacked by fierce, and no doubt bloodthirsty, raiders.

"Ella," said Andy, "it's time we went home, and the quicker the better!"

"That's what I was trying to tell you earlier," Ella said miserably. "I don't know *how* to get back. I'm ever so sorry, Andy, honestly I am, but we're stuck."

CHAPTER VI

The Raiders from the Sea

"THAT'S IT, keep going," Mr. Donkey said encouragingly, "that'll be the last chest that needs shifting, then. I always say it's amazing what you can do when you put your back into it."

Mr. Donkey hadn't actually moved anything himself, since he'd been too busy giving all the orders, but his three unwilling helpers were too tired to point this out to him. There hadn't been any time to be worried, let alone scared, as they had been hustled into the Fort, which in Roman times had held no cozy kitchen or comfortable small bedrooms, let alone apartments. It was just one large, almost empty room with a kind of half-story like an inside balcony, which was reached by a ladder.

On the ground-floor wall there was a row of pegs, on

which hung heavy metal breastplates and large helmets with feathery plumes in them. Ella, who wasn't at all sure of what was going on, wasn't able to resist trying on one of the helmets. It was far too large for her, completely covering her head and resting on her shoulders, and in any other circumstances Andy would have laughed himself silly, but now there was no time.

In a second corner were neatly piled heaps of swords, lances, shields, and daggers, which Andy had carefully avoided looking at, because they somehow seemed to make everything uncomfortably real. He knew that he and Ella belonged in their right place and time in the twentieth century, with washing machines and deep freezes and supermarkets and television. So, of course, it was quite impossible that they might soon be under attack from sea raiders who might take them prisoner or even do something much worse. But all the same, as the three of them struggled to follow Mr. Donkey's directions, he wasn't absolutely certain about this.

The third corner held some large wooden chests and they, in turn, when opened up were full of extremely heavy, thick bags.

"Wages," Mr. Donkey said tersely, "mine included. Three gold pieces a year is all I get, which I call disgraceful. I'm going to ask for a raise after this. It's not right, you know, leaving me with all this responsibility. Now, what's to be done is to shift those bags into the vault. One thing I will say for the Romans, and they are foreign-foreigners, if you follow me, is that they do know a thing or two about security. Watch this, now."

Mr. Donkey went over to the fourth wall, braced himself, and then pushed at the edge of one large stone, which, Andy reckoned, would—or should—be slightly to the left of Mrs. Dunk's stove in nearly two thousand years time. The stone slid sideways to show a deep, dark cupboard.

"Neat, isn't it?" said Mr. Donkey. "Right then, soldier, Tress, and Ella. All those bags are to go in there quick, sharp. I'll tally 'em up as you go."

By the time the last of the money had been safely put away, the sunlight was the goldenred of sunset as it came through the little slit windows, and the bottom of the Fort was full of a filmy golden dust.

"Well done," said Mr. Donkey. "that's that, then. All we've got to do now is to shut up the main door and put the bolts across. It's a shame we can't have anything to eat, but they'd see the smoke if we did. I don't know about you, but I'm quite hungry. Working hard always makes me feel starved. Perhaps there's some cold porridge and a bowl of soup left in the pot. It's over there, Andy, if you'd have a look. I'm tired out, I really am, and . . . "

"The goats!" said Tress suddenly. "The goats are still pegged out."

"You stupid girl!" said Mr. Donkey. "We can't let them raiders get the goats. The centurion'd have my thongs for slings if we lost them, seeing as he only brought them over early summer from some foreign part or other. If we lost the goats he'd deduct the cost from my wages like as not. Hop about, then, it'll be dark in a couple of shakes, and then that lot'll be anchoring off the beach and carrying on something terrible. They'll try to set fire to this and that, but lucky for us the Fort's stone built."

"The front door isn't," Andy pointed out as Tress, hauling up her smock, skipped past them. "Here, I'll come and help you."

"That door's two fists thick," said Mr. Donkey, with just a shade of uncertainty in his voice. "I supposed it *might* burn through, given the time. I wonder now, if it mightn't be better to leave it a little-itty bit open just to show willing? What do you think, soldier?"

Andy wasn't thinking very much at all at this moment, because although his common sense kept telling him that being raided by North Sea people in Roman times really had nothing to do with him and Ella, and that really they must be quite safe, something else was telling him that he was very scared indeed.

What was even worse was that, quite suddenly, he found three pairs of frightened eyes were looking at him in the last golden glow of the sunset, expecting him to know what to do. It was a bit like the time he and his three best friends had found themselves on the wrong bleachers during a big soccer match. They had been horribly outnumbered by opposition supporters and, although it had seemed a cowardly way out, it had been the only sensible course of action. They had run for it.

"Run for it!" said Andy.

They ran.

All four of them bunched together in the doorway for a moment, with Tress slightly in the lead, and then they were hopping, skipping, and in the case of Andy, thumping, over the paving stones and under the arch and up the narrow road.

"I'll probably lose my job, you realize?" said Mr. Donkey, who by now was ahead by several yards. "The centurion'll never give me a good reference after this. Never. Fish, skin, and bones, what's *that!*"

"It's the first of the goats," said Tress breathlessly.

"It gave me a turn," said Mr. Donkey unsteadily, "it looks really nasty in this half-light."

The goat put its head down and definitely snarled, its eyes glittering horribly in the last of the sun's rays. Ella clutched at Andy, who swallowed, but Tress only said calmly, "They're as gentle as lambs, aren't you, my flower? Let Tress untether you then."

And she sank down on her knees and began to struggle with the frayed rope that was fastened to a wooden stake driven into the ground.

"Come on," ordered Mr. Donkey, prodding at the backs of Ella and Andy and pretending that he hadn't been nearly startled out of his skin by the snarling goat. "That centurion gets wild if any foreigners are taken prisoner, and he'll blame it all on me. He always does. There's no fun in being a caretaker, I can tell you. *Now* what are you hanging around for?"

"My duffel coat and socks," said Ella. "Aunt'll be even crosser than your old centurion if I leave them behind. The coat's from Marks and Spencer, and it cost ever such a lot. Yours is over there, Andy. Oh, Andy, I don't like all this. It seems so *real*."

"Marcus and who?" asked Mr. Donkey. "I'm fair winded. I'd never have taken on this post in the first place if I'd've known what it entailed. What I've always wanted is a nice little piece of land farther down the coast, where I could raise ducks and geese and . . . oh!"

The small boat was rapidly getting larger as, with its one

sail billowing, it approached the bay. Just as Mr. Donkey said, "Oh!" a kind of jerky rocket whizzed up from its deck, shot into the air, and then landed just short of the Fort on the sand. It spluttered fitfully, sending up a shower of sparks, and then fizzed and went out.

"Whatever next?" said Mr. Donkey. "They'll be using one of those catapult machines. That's not playing by the rules at all. Well, I'd better see to the goats on the other side of the hill. There's no knowing where all this is going to end. See you soon . . ."

And with an astonishing burst of speed, Mr. Donkey clambered up the hillside and vanished into the lengthening shadows.

"I want to go home," said Ella in a small voice, "and I want to go home *now*."

It was on the tip of Andy's tongue to say that he did, too, and, anyway, it was Ella who had got them into this frightening situation in the first place, when a second fireball exploded from the raiders' boat. This one landed fair and square on the roof of the Fort, slid down it spluttering and fizzing, and then came to rest briefly on the broken guttering, which promptly tipped it onto the paving stones, where it slowly and reluctantly went out.

By this time the sea was a molten red and the reflected sunlight coming off it was so dazzling that neither Andy nor Ella had noticed that two small rowboats had left the raiders' ship and were coming in to land. The men in them were wearing enormous helmets with great horns sticking out of them, furry jackets and boots, and were carrying very sharp spears. In a hairy kind of way they were not unlike the goats to look at.

"Oh, dear. I wish Aunt were here," said Ella loudly.

"Maa-maa-maa," replied a number of voices even more loudly, and right behind them.

"What's that?" asked Ella, clutching at Andy's coat, which he was half in and half out of.

"Goats, you idiot."

His bad leg was starting to throb and itch again, he was getting more frightened by the minute, and he hadn't the least idea what to do next, so he shoved his hands into his pockets and took a deep breath. What could he, Andy Jones, of the twentieth century, do about North Sea pirates who were about to burn down a Roman fort? It probably had nothing to do with him if they *did*, of course. What was really important was, how was he going to get Ella and himself back safe and sound to the time and place where they belonged?

Then about three things happened at once. The first was that he heard Tress's shrill, terrified voice shout, "Rescue, help, rescue...."

The second was that his left hand closed over the old pocketknife (one blade broken) that he always carried with him, and the third was that his right hand was now grasping the soccer rattle with which he encouraged his team from their side of the bleachers.

"Hang on," said Andy, "those raiders are creeping up the hill and they've nearly got to Tress. She's got her foot caught in a tether. Well, they're not going to get her. Ella, here's my knife. It's sharp, so watch it. Go and cut the rest of those goats free."

"I don't like goats."

"They're as mild as lambs, Tress said so and she should know. Anyway, they're a hundred times nicer than the raiders. The goats won't hurt you, honestly. And if you want to get back to Aunt, this'll be the only way. Now hurry."

"All right," Ella said in a grumbling voice, "all right, but if they step on me or butt me I'll tell Aunt."

With the knife in one hand Ella crawled off on all fours. She was trembling as she approached the first goat, but she made herself go on, because she hadn't liked the way in which her "twin" had shouted for help, and if her "twin" really was in danger of being captured, then it was up to her, Ella, to save her.

"Nice, um, nice goaty . . ."

The goat put down its hideous head and rubbed it gently against Ella's trembling hands.

"Right," said Andy, "well, here goes then. It's us against them. Tress is down there and the raiders have got her, or they've nearly got her, *and* they've reached the Fort."

A gentle blue dusk was falling over the hillside, which was strangely quiet, as if all the wildlife were waiting for something terrible to happen. The only signs of life were the flaring torches held by the invaders, who were now crossing the Fort and climbing up the path to where Tress was lying in the bracken, too scared to move.

"Rescue," whispered Andy. He took a deep breath, forgot about his aching leg, and pulled himself to his feet. He glanced at Ella, who had just finished hacking through the last tether and was now surrounded by goats, who were all nudging and hinting that it was high time that they got down to the Fort. Andy pulled his right hand out of the pocket of his coat, held it above his head, and whirled it around and around.

In the still, clear air of nearly two thousand years ago it was quite amazing how much noise a twentieth-century soccer rattle made. Skylarks, pigeons, oyster catchers, gulls, rats, moles, voles, mice, hedgehogs, and every other living creature above and below ground panicked. Even the guillemots, shags, and cormorants far out to sea took to their wings and came sweeping out of their rocky homes. As for the goats, they just couldn't get away from the awful noise fast enough, and in a terrified bleeting, baaing, maaing mass they started to career down the hill.

"Rescue! Rescue! *Rescue!*" roared Andy, swinging the soccer rattle at full pitch.

The very last glimmer of the blood red shone in the goats' eyes as they rampaged through the bracken. The light turned their curling horns to gold and their long fleeces to a deep, ruddy red. The raiders who were all standing as still as tombstones as they stared up at the hill, felt their blood turn cold. With their shaggy coats and horned helmets they felt as if they were seeing their own avenging spirits bearing down on them out of the mist. They were brave enough in ordinary battle, but they were also chockful of superstition, and one by one they felt a terrible fear take hold of them, so that they could no longer grasp their spears and shields.

CLATTER CLATTER CLATTER went the rattle.

"RESCUE!" roared Andy and Ella together.

"BAAA-MAAAH," went the goats.

There was a moment's pause, and then the raiders of one accord turned and ran as fast as their furry boots would carry them back to the shore and the safety of their boats.

"RESCUE, RESCUE, RESCUE," shouted Andy, who by now was quite carried away by what was happening as he urged on his "troops." Then he caught his bad leg in a trailing bramble and went down head over heels. Everything seemed to turn the colors of the rainbow and then very dark indeed.

When Andy managed to open his eyes after a very, very long time, he saw two faces looking down at him. One belonged to Tress and the other to a man he had never seen before, who was wearing the same kind of helmet with feathers in it that Ella had tried on earlier. It was a nice, square, sensible sort of face and it was saying, "He's coming around."

"Um," mumbled Andy, who was feeling rather sick.

"I understand from the Lady Tress that we have a great deal to thank you for," said the centurion, his eyes twinkling. "I only regret that we have arrived too late to see you leading your, er, army into action. It was nobly done, Hadrian, and we thank you."

"That's all right," mumbled Andy, who was still feeling far from well.

"One day I hope that we, or I alone, may repay the debt we owe you for saving our new fort."

"And thank you, too, my flower," said Tress, "for rescuing me. A proper wounded knight come to my aid, you were. But now it's time that you . . ."

"Yes, but what about Ella and . . ."

"I think he's going to faint again," the centurion's voice said as Andy closed his eyes.

"No, no," said Tress softly, "he's going to sleep, to sleep, to sleep . . ."

"But what about . . ." Andy began, but before he could finish what he meant to say he felt himself falling into a great, spinning darkness of silence.

CHAPTER VII

The Rescue
of Mervyn

WHEN ANDY woke up again for the second time he did so rather slowly, because he dimly remembered that something very unpleasant had happened. What it was he couldn't quite recall for a moment or two, and then everything came back with a rush and he sat bolt upright. Lolly, who had been dozing happily on his chest, fell onto the floor, twitched her whiskers at him, and stalked off with her tail up.

"Better now?" asked Mrs. Tressida, who was sitting in front of the fire. "Ella's gone to get the tea. She's been telling me about your adventures. You *have* been busy."

"We're back?" asked Andy cautiously. "Both of us? Right place? Right time?"

"Yes."

Andy blew out his cheeks and sank back on the sofa. Moving around in time was, he decided, just as tiring as traveling in space, and it took some getting used to.

"At least I've stopped feeling sick," he said at last, "and my leg doesn't ache, either. Did we really go into Roman times?"

"So it would seem from all accounts. What did you think of them?"

Andy shifted his bad leg and put his hands behind his head. Lolly sprang lightly onto the back of the sofa and walked down his shoulder and onto his stomach, turned around and around, and then settled comfortably with her eyes fixed unblinkingly on Andy's face.

"It was—it was interesting," Andy said slowly, "and it was funny seeing the island being joined to the mainland like that. What happened to the R. Twelve?"

"It was the Sea People. They got more and more self-important, saying that this, that, and the other was their territory. Reclaiming what was rightly theirs, they called it. Lot of nonsense! They were just being greedy. Old Neap, well Young Neap he was then, got his people to nibble away at the R. Twelve deep down and then, when he'd got it nice and shaky, he started to blow up some storms. Storms and a half they were, too. This place stood firm, of course, because it's Roman built, but a lot of the Forelanders lost their wooden houses. A part of the old causeway's still there under the water, and at very low tide you can see it yet. And there's bits and pieces of it down on the sand, all mixed up with the rocks. It's sad in a way when you remember that once upon a time it ran straight as a ruler all the way to middle Rome."

Mrs. Tressida sighed, her little puckered face lighted by the leaping flames.

"Go on," Andy said, stroking Lolly behind one ear so that she started a deep, rumbling purr of pleasure.

"Well, it was *my* gateway to freedom gone, although I didn't realize it at the time, being young and foolish. Of course, once the causeway was broken, there I was caught fast on the island—as it had become. Old Neap's a greedy one, I can tell you. He hasn't changed at all, and he's still nibbling away at islands and countries and continents and coastlines all over the world. It's being greedy for power that's at the bottom of most of the mischief in the world."

"Did the raiders come back again?"

"Bless you, they stopped a little while and then, bold as bold they came again. And after them came the ships from the Lowlands, not to mention the pirates who hailed from no country in particular. If the truth be told, it got so bad about three or four hundred years ago that the islanders took to having lookouts posted during the raiding season. Of course, to be fair, it has to be said that by then a number of the islanders had taken to the sea themselves to pick up a living. Free trading *they* called it, but when it comes down to it, it was smuggling."

"Yes, but look here," said Andy, trying to stick to a particular point, although he wanted to hear a lot more about the pirates and smugglers. "How did Ella and I get back *here*?"

"Oh, that Tress wasn't as green as she was cabbage-looking," said Mrs. Tressida with a chuckle. "She'd called you up for help, so I hear, and you gave it to her, so in return for that favor she brought you and Ella home safe and sound. It was a close-run thing, my flower, but she managed it. Just!"

"Tea," said Ella, coming in backward through the door because she was carrying a very large tray. "Are you hungry, Andy?"'

"Starving," said Andy. "I'll tell you what, there's nothing like exploring and hiding treasures and being attacked by raiders and all that for making you hungry. Mrs. Tressida, can I ask you a few more questions, please?"

"Fish, skin, and bones, do. Have a peanut-butter sandwich. Ella, pour out the tea."

By unspoken consent Andy and Ella both decided to give magic a rest for the next few days. They talked over and over all that had happended on that summer day in Roman times and Ella described how the North Sea men had rowed back to their mother ship which had been anchored out in the bay.

"There were goats everywhere," said Ella, not looking worried for once as she talked with her chin on her knees. "And you were just lying there looking awful and I thought you were dead, but Tress said, 'Nonsense, he's just knocked out in the head. Come on, we'll get him back to the Fort. I'll take his arms and you take his legs.' You weigh an awful lot, Andy, particularly your bad leg, you know.

"Well, anyway, we got you down to the beach somehow, and by the time we reached the Fort the front door had stopped burning, but there was an awful smell of charred wood and there was smoke and goats everywhere. Tress was running around trying to calm them down and she was

in an awful state about losing her job as a goatherd, and I
didn't know what to do at all. I knew it was an adventure
and all that, but I'm not brave, and really I was quite
scared, because it was nighttime and ever so dark and the
North Sea men's boat was still out in the bay. They'd hung a
lantern on the sharp end of it and I kept thinking that they
might be coming back and . . ."

"Go on," said Andy, picking up a flat stone and throwing
it sideways at the calm winter sea. The stone bounced three
times and then vanished with a plop.

"And, well, then suddenly Mr. Donkey came back. He
said he'd decided that after all he should look after the Fort,
no matter what the cost might be . . ."

"He didn't!" said Andy, starting to laugh.

"He did! And he was telling Tress how to catch the goats,
only he didn't catch any of them himself."

"Oh, oh, oh," said Andy, who by this time was doubled
up with laughter. "Oh, I do wish I'd been there. I mean, I
know I was, but I didn't know I was because of being
knocked out. I can just imagine what it was like with you
and Tress running around in the dark trying to get hold of
the goats and Mr. Donkey giving all the orders. Oh, oh, oh."

"It may seem funny to you," said Ella, with her chin up in
the air, "but it wasn't funny to us. Especially me, because I
didn't want to stay there for ever and ever. And then
suddenly Mr. Donkey said, 'Look, what's that, then?' and
we saw a whole long line of lights coming across the causeway and we heard the sound of marching, and a few
minutes later the lantern was turned off on the raiders' ship
and Mr. Donkey said, 'They're off! They won't be back in a

hurry. They've learned their lesson. We Forelanders *always* defeat the North Sea men. Just listen to their oars going."

"Then what?"

"Oh, the North Sea men rowed away and Tress and I had just got most of the goats into the sheds when this nice Roman man arrived. 'Great Jumping Jupiter,' he said, or something like that. 'One of my men on scout duty came galloping across the causeway to my camp saying there was a Northman ship harbored off the Fort, and that the Fort itself was under fire. So, of course, I ordered my troops to return at the double, only to discover that there are no invaders, no ships, and no fire. So would one of you be good enough to tell me exactly what *has* been going on?' Tress and Mr. Donkey and I all tried to explain and I suppose it was a bit muddled because the goats kept butting in, but he seemed to work it out somehow and then you woke up. You remember that, don't you?"

"Yes, sort of," said Andy, skimming another stone, which did four bounces this time.

"Well, then this nice Roman man, who was really the captain of the Fort, asked Tress if she couldn't help us to get home. And she got out her crystal and did a spell and everything went misty and the next thing was that we were back here in the proper Fort and Aunt was just waking up from her sleep. Only . . ."

"Only what?"

"Nothing. Only that it's very nice to be back. I liked Tress, didn't you? Even if she was a bit bossy. I'm glad she was rescued. How do you make stones bounce like that?"

It was very pleasant to skim pebbles, to clamber over the

sand dunes, and to explore as much of the rocks as Andy's cast would let him. They had Tommy with them since Mr. Dunk had said he was too busy trying to mend the electric light, which had mysteriously fused quite suddenly. Ella had been in the Dunks's kitchen when it happened, and as the lights flickered on and off, Andy had looked at her and mouthed silently, "Aunt."

Ella had choked and then become very busy doing up the clasps on her duffel coat.

"You know," said Andy, thinking of this now and throwing a piece of wood for Tommy to chase, "it can't go on like this with all the electrical things going wrong. Mr. and Mrs. Dunk are bound to catch on."

"No, they won't. Grown-up people don't believe in magic. Except for Aunt, of course, and it's different for her because she's a witch. Doing magic is fun. Why don't you learn some?"

"No, thanks," said Andy firmly. "Trying to think of ways of rescuing Aunt is enough for me. Here, Tommy, good dog, give me the wood."

Tommy stood still for a moment, raised one paw, and then bounded off with the wood still in his mouth.

"He's about the silliest dog I've ever met," said Andy with disgust. "Here, that reminds me, what's happened to Mervyn? Where does he live?"

"Who? Oh, oh, *Mervyn*," Ella's face reddened. "Oh, he lives on the other side of the rocks."

"But there isn't a house there."

"Yes, well, you see . . ."

"Go on."

"I can't. It's secret."

"Now, look here," said Andy, who was practically glowing like a candle with curiosity by this time, "I was the one who rescued Mervyn from Tommy and I got knocked about doing it. You've got to tell me what's going on."

"I can't, I can't, I can't. I wish I could, but I can't!"

Ella scrambled off the rock on which she was perched and ran off down the beach as though there were a force-ten gale behind her. Tommy thought this was some wonderful new game and went racing after her, barking and jumping up and down and turning a complete somersault as a posse of sea gulls went whirling and squawking up into the gray sky.

"Girls!" said Andy. He began to examine the rocks, which had once been the end part of the R.XII that led to Rome. Although Old Neap and nearly two thousand years of weather had done their best to destroy the causeway, it was still possible to see that underneath the thick covering of seaweed there were some man-made flagstones.

"It's funny to think that history's real," Andy said to no one in particular, as he carefully removed a tiny white crab that had come out of the seaweed and was now trying, in a somewhat distracted way, to run up his sleeve.

"Looking for bait?" asked a voice from behind him.

Andy turned and looked over his shoulder and up at a square-faced stranger, who was wearing a shiny yellow jacket and trousers and a woolen hat and was carrying a fishing rod.

"No, looking at the old causeway."

"That, if you don't mind my saying so, is an old wives' tale," said the stranger.

"No, it isn't. I *know* it isn't. I mean," Andy added hastily, "there are still bits of it here, like these stones."

"Oh, *those*." The man leaned against the rocks and smiled. "They're old, all right, I grant you. Roman probably. But they were moved here much later to make a slipway, a kind of path for people to walk down to reach their boats. This was the island's main harbor, you see, up till about two hundred years ago, and then the whole bay began to silt up with sand, so they had to build a harbor on the other side of the island."

Andy said nothing, but he looked disbelieving and the stranger laughed.

"All right," he said, "have it your way. You're new here, aren't you? I don't seem to know your face."

Andy explained himself and the man nodded and unzipped one of his pockets. He took out a pipe and lighted it and, as the flame from his lighter plopped up and down in the gathering dusk, Andy began to have that strange, tingling feeling on his fingers and toes again, which he now knew meant that there was some curious magic about. The last time he had seen a face very like the stranger's was by the flickering flames of a torch. Only then the face had been topped by a great, shining helmet with feathers in it. . . .

". . .hope you'll enjoy your stay," the man was saying. "Do you know, it's odd, but although we've never met I'm sure I've seen you somewhere before. We've probably sat opposite each other in a train or bus or something on the mainland. Please give my regards to Mr. and Mrs. Dunk. My name is Remuson, by the way. And if you'd ever like to come out fishing, get in touch with me and, if it's possible,

I'll take you with me on my boat. Are you a good sailor?"

"I don't know, I've never been in a boat."

"Well, you should try it. It's great fun. My word, the tide's coming in fast. You'd better get back to the Fort or you might find yourself in difficulties."

Andy watched Mr. Remuson walk away and then began to plod back to the Fort as the sea, with a slight wind behind it, started to ripple hungrily across the sand, pushing the little swaths of weed ahead of it.

The tingling feeling was still with him and he didn't think he liked it all that much, because it made him feel uneasy. Suddenly he decided that it would be a good idea if he telephoned his mother at work and made sure that everything was all right at home. If the phone was working, of course.

"Mr. Remuson!" said Mrs. Dunk. "Well, fancy—"

"That," agreed Mr. Dunk. "Nice man. Very nice man. He's our landlord, you see. He owns the Fort. I hope you didn't tell him about our little trouble with the TV and the lights and all the rest of it? No, of course you didn't. Well, we've got no problems at the moment. Touch wood and whistle. I've been working and working away all the afternoon."

"He put in a new fuse," Mrs. Dunk said proudly as she rattled knives, forks, and spoons on to the kitchen table. "And Tommy did have a lovely."

"Run. Fair worn out when he got back. But that little Ella, she was pale as pale could be. Terrible little worrier she is. My word, it's shepherd's pie, which is one of my favorites. And there's a good cowboy film on the TV tonight.

If you want to call your mother, you'd better get on with it, Andy, or I'll have your helping of pie as well as my own. All that hard work's given me a real appetite. My word, the wind's getting up a bit. Well, it's bound to do that at this time of year, and as I'm always saying to Mrs. Dunk..."

Andy's mother sounded very bright and cheerful on the phone, and she told him several times over that everything at work was lovely and that she was glad he was enjoying himself and that he'd settled in so well at the island.

"What about the kitchen ceiling?" asked Andy, standing on one foot in the passage and sniffing at the delicious smell that was stealing out of the kitchen.

"Well, it has got a *little* bit larger," his mother's voice said in his ear, "but it's nothing to worry about. I've written to the Horrible Landlord about it and... Andy, are you there, dear? All I can hear is a crackling, buzzing sound. Andy? Andy?"

"It's all because of Aunt," Andy shouted.

"Yes, dear, very faint. Call again next week. 'Bye, dear."

Andy put down the phone and thumped into the kitchen, where Mr. Dunk was already halfway through his helping of pie and talking away with his mouth full.

"The wind's come around a bit," he said to Andy. "Have some cabbage in onion sauce. I'm glad to know that you've made friends with Mr. Remuson. His family has lived on the island for hundreds of years, almost as long as my family, in fact. Is there any more cabbage? Thanks. You're looking better already, Andy. You're not half as pale as when you arrived. What's for dessert?"

In spite of all the problems and questions on his mind,

Andy fell fast asleep within a couple of minutes of getting into bed that night and then, quite suddenly, he was wide awake again. He didn't know what it was that had woken him up, though. The call of a night bird, or the thin, high moan of the wind, or the sound of the slapping waves just below his window. Or even something calling inside his own head and saying, "Rescue, rescue, rescue . . ."

"Oh, not *again!*" said Andy and slid out of bed. He pulled on his duffel coat feeling cross and fuzz-headed and picking up his flashlight, he made his way as quietly as he could down the stairs, through the kitchen, and out the front door.

The wind was very cold as it plucked at his coat, and Andy, who was in a very bad mood, was just about to climb up the steep stone steps to Aunt's door to see what was the matter *now*, when he realized that the irritating voice that was buzzing in his ears was coming from outside the Fort.

"Oh, no," Andy muttered, "*now* what's happened?"

Thumping and snorting, he made his way under the arch and then turned right. His eyes had gotten used to the dark by now, and in the increasingly bright starlight he could make out that the sea was licking right over the sand to its high-tide mark. Two round yellow eyes swooped out of the night sky and then vanished into the cold darkness.

"Rescue, rescue, rescue . . ." said the voice.

"Rescue WHAT?" snapped Andy.

All he could see were the cold, curling dark waves splashing over the gray-white sand and a couple of shadowy shapes that could have been mounds of seaweed.

"Andy?" said Ella's voice.

"Yes," Andy said furiously. "What is it *now*?"

"It's . . ." Ella swallowed, "it's what I couldn't tell you about before because of it being a secret. Only it's not a secret anymore. It's Mervyn."

The second dark shape moved and the pale greeny-gray face of Mervyn came into focus in the moonlight, his green eyes glittering.

"I've escaped," Mervyn said, "got out, made a swim for it, and I need help. Ella can't manage, so I had to ask her to call you. I didn't want to do it, but I had to because they'll be after me any minute now."

"I *couldn't* ask Aunt to help," said Ella. "I'd told Mervyn I would, but I couldn't, because he's . . . well, he's . . ."

Mervyn hoisted himself up onto his arms and dragged himself out of the shadows. Andy watched him do it and he could feel his eyes goggling because, as the rest of Mervyn came into view, one thing was extremely obvious. Mervyn was a perfectly ordinary boy as far as his waist, but then . . .

"He's one of the Sea People," Ella whispered, "and he wants to get away from them, because he wants to be a land person and have proper legs and not a tail. You will help him, Andy, won't you?"

"Of course, if you can't help me, I'll quite understand," said Mervyn gruffly, flicking his tail over the sand.

"I . . . I . . . I . . ." said Andy, who was staring at the merboy as if he were hyptonized. Then, even as he tried to speak, from deep inside the Fort there came the most awful, bloodcurdling, howling noise.

"It's Tommy!" said Andy, Ella, and Mervyn all together.

"Come on, quick," said Andy. "We've only got a couple of minutes at the most. Ella, you take his arms and I'll take his tail, and for goodness' sake get a move on."

CHAPTER VIII

Mervyn
Vanishes

"UP THE STAIRS," panted Ella, "we'll have to use the second apartment. It's empty and it's not locked."

Mervyn wasn't very large, but he seemed to weigh a ton as Andy and Ella struggled to get him up the crumbling steps, and an added difficulty was that his tail was extremely slippery. One moment Andy thought he had it tight, and then the next it had slid through his hands and was whacking against the stonework. They had just reached the wooden door when a gold square of light fell across the dark, weedy courtyard.

"It's Mr. Dunk," Andy said, wheezing and gasping. "If he lets Tommy out, we'll be in the soup."

Tommy was baying and howling away like mad, and from

the thud, thud, thud noise down below it sounded as if he were throwing himself against the front door in an effort to get out.

"Stupid dog!" shouted Mr. Dunk. "What do you mean by it? Quiet! Quiet, I say! Waking us all up like this, you should be ashamed of yourself."

"Yooooow," howled Tommy.

"Quiet, I say."

"Yooooow."

"Stupid animal. Here, have a chocky-doggy-bikkey and SHUT UP!"

The three upstairs in the top apartment held their breaths—and then let them go again as the howling stopped and a moment later the light vanished.

"Better give Mr. Dunk a moment or two," whispered Andy, "and then I'll turn on my flashlight."

"Better not," Mervyn whispered back. "I can see in the dark anyway, because it gets very dark underwater, you know. And if *you* wait a moment or two, we could be in awful trouble. I'm sorry about all this, but I had to get away tonight. They've been suspicious for a long time, but this evening I knew that *they* knew about me, so, when they were busy and nobody was looking in my direction, I made a dash for it. I put out an S.O.S. for help to Ella. . . . "

"Yes, I heard you at once," Ella said. "I had the little crystal by my bed and it was just like an alarm clock going off. But I don't know how Andy heard it."

"It was in my head," Andy said, "but what I don't understand is why, if you're a Sea Person, you want to escape."

"It's a long story," said Mervyn, switching his tail backward and forward across the dusty floorboards and leaving tracks in the moonlight. "I hate to mention it, but I'm starting to feel a bit itchy. Is there any water anywhere?"

"There's the bathtub," suggested Ella.

As quietly as they could, they hauled Mervyn into the bathroom and turned on the cold tap. Both Andy and Ella had gotten used to the darkness by now, and once the bathtub was half full of cold water they pushed and pulled Mervyn into it. He lay under the water for a minute or so and then hauled himself up into sitting position, his green eyes shining like emeralds.

"That's better, thanks," he said, flipping his tail up and down gently.

"Why do you want to escape?" Andy persisted.

"It all began a long time ago," Mervyn replied and yawned. There's nothing more catching than yawning, so Andy and Ella found themselves doing the same thing.

"I tell you what," said Mervyn, "I'm tired and so are you. Supposing I explain in the morning?"

Andy hesitated and then went over to the window. It was extremely dirty, and he breathed on the glass and then polished it with his sleeves. The sky was dark, with a lot of scudding white clouds flying across the cold winter moon. It was as if a silvery light were being turned on and off, and in one of the "on" moments Andy thought he could see some dark shapes humping their way toward the shore through the frothing waves. He pressed his nose against the glass, trying to see better, and at once it misted up.

"Darn," he muttered and wiped the window again, but by the time it was fairly clear, there was nothing to be seen except sky, sand, and sea.

"What is it?" Ella asked sharply.

"Nothing. Just looking."

Andy glanced past her to Mervyn, whose eyes seemed to sparkle with green light in the shadows.

"Are you sure you'll be safe here?" Andy said.

"Oh, yes," Mervyn said after a split second's hesitation. "I'm on dry land. In fact," he added proudly, sending up little drops of water with a swish of his tail, "I'm the only Sea Person I've heard of who's been properly ashore. Thanks very much for rescuing me and now if you don't mind. . . ." And he gave another enormous yawn and slid slowly under the water until he was lying on the bottom of the bathtub.

Ella and Andy tiptoed out of the bathroom and through the apartment, which was so cold that they could hear each other's teeth chattering.

"I'm ever so sorry, getting you into this," said Ella, blowing on her hands as they shut the front door. "But I didn't know what to do and I was so worried and I couldn't tell Aunt and . . ."

"It's okay," said Andy, who was very, very worried indeed himself. "See you in the morning. It'll be all right."

But he crossed his fingers behind his back as he spoke. It was very flattering to be called a "wounded knight" who was going to rescue people all over the place; but as far as he could make out, matters were going from bad to worse at a horrifying speed. He still didn't have the least idea how to transport Mrs. Tressida back to the mainland, he had an extremely nasty feeling that the Sea People were somehow going to kidnap Mervyn, and, worst of all, he hadn't liked the way his mother had been so bright and cheerful on the phone, because he knew from experience that it meant she was covering up something unpleasant.

Nevertheless, in spite of all these problems, Andy fell deeply asleep the moment he climbed back into bed, and he was still fast asleep when Mr. Dunk hammered on the door and came striding into the room and thumped himself down on Andy's bed.

"It's all right for some," said Mr. Dunk in an aggrieved voice, "sleeping their heads off while others are working. There was me up half the night with Tommy barking fit to bust. He's a very clever dog, is Tommy. We had a prowler around the Fort last night."

Andy was suddenly very wide awake, with all kinds of ideas flashing through his head like a pinball machine lighting up. Tommy had followed Mervyn's tracks, traced him up the stone stairs, and tracked him to the bathtub. Mervyn had been discovered and cross-examined and . . .

"Funny, you wearing your duffel coat in bed," said Mr. Dunk, "you'd better ask Mrs. Dunk for another blanket if you're cold, you know."

"I—"

"Yes, a prowler," said Mr. Dunk, getting up so suddenly that all the bedsprings went "woooing" and Andy nearly rolled onto the floor. "Came right up to the main door of the Fort, he did, and left his prints all over the place. I wouldn't be surprised if there was more than one at that, seeing as how the sand is all disturbed and my van's pushed over to one side. It's not right. I can't deal with prowlers *and* look after the Fort. It's asking too much and I've a good mind to tell Mr. Remuson so. I said to Mrs. Dunk, I said, I'd hand in my notice tomorrow and move to the mainland and buy a nice little small property. Mrs. Dunk agreed with me. It's haddock for breakfast. Only we haven't got the money. Shake a leg, soldier."

Both Tommy and Mr. Dunk looked very heavy-eyed after breakfast, and the pair of them, with their paws and hands crossed, were having a nice little nap by the time Andy had finished helping Mrs. Dunk wash the breakfast things.

"Don't you *like* haddock, Andy?" asked Mrs. Dunk, as she scurried around the kitchen with a broom, carefully avoiding Tommy and Mr. Dunk, who looked remarkably alike as they snored with their mouths open. "Haddock is very good for."

"You. Me, I mean," agreed Andy. "Yes, it was very nice. I'll just put this piece on a plate and have it later, if that's okay."

"There's a good boy," said Mrs. Dunk, swishing past him. "Well, I'll just go and clean upstairs and then I'm off to do the."

"Shopping?" suggested Andy, but Mrs. Dunk had already scuttled up the stairs.

"Phew," said Andy as he carefully scooped the rest of the haddock into a paper bag. It occurred to him that Mervyn, after his dramatic swim for freedom, might be hungry.

"Going to see Ella," Andy said, as he caught up with Mrs. Dunk, who was scrubbing out the bathtub with so much enthusiasm that the cleanser was going in all directions like a miniature snowstorm.

"That's nice. Get her shopping list from her, will you, Andy? I do their shopping for them, since Mrs. Tressida doesn't like riding on the bus. It makes her feel unwell, she says. Poor old lady."

"Yes, okay."

Andy limped out of the Fort and across the courtyard, noticing as he did so how much the sand had been disturbed. Quite close to Mr. Dunk's van he saw a distinct print of what looked like a large, fishy fin.

"Sugar!" said Andy, with a cold shiver going up his back. It looked very much as if the Sea People, in spite of what Mervyn had said, were quite capable of coming rather a long way inshore—if they got this far. It also explained "the prowler"!

Andy rubbed his plastered foot backward and forward over the sand to wipe out the print. Somehow it seemed to make last night's adventure seem uncomfortably close and, although the wind was very cold, Andy felt as if he were sweating as he climbed the stone stairs.

"There you are, dear," said Mrs. Tressida, who was sitting in front of the fire with Lolly fast asleep in her lap. "Did you hear the wind in the night, my flower? Gusting it was and it woke me up. I did have a very uneasy night altogether, because I suddenly had the feeling that there were Sea People around. There was something in the air . . . but doubtless it's all nonsense. When you get to my age you imagine all sorts of strange things. Now what's the matter with you, standing there with your mouth open. Kitten-cat got your tongue?"

Andy shut his mouth with a snap and pulled himself together. Just for a split second Mrs. Tressida had made him think of somebody else, but who that somebody could be he hadn't the faintest idea.

"Shopping list?" he said, saying the first words that came into his mind. "Mrs. Dunk asked for it."

"It's here," Mrs. Tressida replied, hauling a piece of paper out from underneath Lolly, who sighed and turned over and then went instantly to sleep again. "Mrs. Dunk's a kind soul. I don't know where Ella's got to. It's a strange thing. Andy, but I can quite definitely smell *fish!*"

"It was haddock for breakfast," gulped Andy, and then made off as quickly as his bad leg would carry him. What with making his bed and giving Mr. Dunk a hand with lifting a ladder, it was nearly half an hour before Andy managed to get to the front door of the "empty" apartment.

"Hey! Anyone home?" Andy asked softly.

There was no reply except from the chilly whistling of the wind around the roof of the Fort, and the distant booming of the sea.

"Ella?" Andy called more loudly.

A door banged somewhere and Andy peered around the edge of the stairway and saw Mrs. Dunk, an empty shopping bag in either hand, go hurrying off under the stone arch toward the road. The blue island bus came around the far headland and it and Mrs. Dunk met at the corner. Andy forgot all his worries for a moment, as he remembered what this part of the island had looked like nearly two thousand years ago. It was strange to realize that then the road had been a great deal smoother and better built than it was now. Immediately below him had been the wooden stables and the goat pens, and the hill behind the summer house had been covered with the shaggy beasts.

What was more, now that the sea was going out fast in little choppy gray waves, he could see a sort of shadowy outline of the old causeway, with one small fishing boat tossing up and down as it tried to find a way around the end of the island to the harbor.

"Glad I'm not on board it," Andy said to himself. "It's bobbing up and down like a cork. It must be really rough out there. I wonder why, because the wind's died down quite a bit. I suppose the R. Twelve underwater makes it full of currents."

He got so interested in watching what was happening to the distant sailing boat that he quite forgot for a moment or two that he was supposed to be looking for Ella and Mervyn, until the door at his elbow was thrown open and a furious voice said, "Oh, *there* you are! Well, don't just stand mooning about with your mouth half open. Where have you been? You do smell fishy."

"Got some haddock for Mervyn's breakfast. What are you so cross about?"

"Cross? *I'm* not cross," replied Ella furiously, trying to push the hair out of her eyes and practically jumping up and down in her agitation. "I'm just . . . oh, come on."

She caught hold of Andy's sleeve and dragged him into the empty apartment. By daylight it didn't look like a very nice place: There were patches of damp on the walls, and all the furniture was piled up together in the middle of the rooms. It was also extremely cold.

"There," said Ella, throwing open a door. "There, what do you think of that?"

It was the bathroom they had been in last night and the first thing Andy noticed was the clean patch he had made on the window, and the second was that although the bathtub was still half full of water, it was otherwise empty, apart from some sand and mud in the bottom. Andy stared at it and then turned to look at Ella, who was standing with her hands on her waist and her chin up.

"Where is he?" said Andy.

"*I* don't know," said Ella. "All *I* know is that he's gone. Vanished. The Sea People must have come ashore in the middle of the night and climbed up the stairs and captured him. Look, there are marks all over the floor!"

Andy sat down on the edge of the bathtub to rest his leg and stared at Ella, who stared straight back at him.

"Well," said Ella, "*you're* the wounded knight. You're the one who is supposed to rescue everybody, so what are you going to do now?"

Dimly Andy remembered how ages and ages ago his mother had kept on telling him that it wasn't everybody who was lucky enough to be going to spend their vacation on an island. And, at this particular moment, in the ugly, freezing little apartment under the roof of the Fort, he would almost have been quite glad *not* to be lucky. And then, to his own great surprise, he heard himself say, "What I'm going to do is follow the marks, because they'll lead us to Mervyn. Come on, or has the catfish got your tongue?"

CHAPTER IX

The Police
and the Prowler

THE TAILPRINTS that Mervyn had left behind him on the dusty floor were easy to follow. They led out of the bathroom, down the narrow passage, and into a poky little room right under the eaves. It was very dark and shadowy, since it only had one tiny window, which was about eight inches square and extremely dirty. Andy tried the electric switch, which naturally didn't work, and then bravely hobbled across to clean the window with his cuff. In spite of everything else that was on his mind, it struck him as an odd sort of window, unlike any that he had ever seen before. Through it he could just see, not the bay, but to the right of it and up to the dark headland beneath which the raiders' boat had once anchored.

"Andy?" said a thin whisper from the doorway. "Are you all right? Is he there? What's that noise?"

Andy hadn't noticed the noise until then, because it was all mixed up with the distant thudding of the sea and the moaning of the wind. But now he became aware that there was another quite different sound in the little room. It was a distinct "glug-glug-plop" and it was right behind him. He felt the hairs rise on the back of his neck as his imagination conjured up a giant jellyfish or some hideous deep-sea "thing" watching him from the shadows in the corner. His very sweaty hand reached into his coat pocket for a weapon and came out with his flashlight, which he had forgotten all about.

The yellow beam of light flashed across the dingy darkness and came to rest on a rusty water tank. The ball cock wasn't working very well and it seemed to be struggling for its life as it bobbed up and down and gulped.

"It's j-just an old t-tank," Andy said, "n-nothing to be scared of. Come in, Mervyn must be here somewhere."

Ella tiptoed in reluctantly, her face as pale as a ghost's in the gloom. Together they watched the wavering beam of the flashlight—which still wasn't too steady in Andy's hand—as it picked out Mervyn's tail-trail to where it reached the tank and then stopped.

"He must be in there," said Ella, keeping very close behind Andy.

"Well, at least he can't be drowned."

Andy shone the flashlight down into the murky depths. The water wasn't very clean, but even so they could see to the bottom of the tank and Mervyn definitely wasn't in it.

"Do you think Sea People can vanish?" Ella buzzed in Andy's ear.

"I don't know," Andy said crossly, "and don't *do* that, it makes my ear twitch."

Fortunately it hadn't occurred to Ella, as it had to Andy, that one reason why Mervyn seemed to have disappeared into thin, if dusty, air, might be because he had been recaptured.

"Hang on to my coat."

Ella hung on, while Andy, sounding a great deal braver than he really felt, said, "There's a gap between the back of the tank and the wall. Perhaps there's a cupboard there or something."

Andy balanced his stomach on the rim of the tank and, feeling very unsafe, shone the flashlight on the back wall. What he saw nearly made him tip over into the dusty water. He could just make out a very tattered old piece of hardboard, which had once been badly nailed over a hole in the stonework. Only now the hardboard had come un-nailed and the crumbling hole was all too obvious.

"Mervyn!" shouted Andy. "Are you down there?"

There was a long pause and then a very tired, faint voice replied. "All right, I give myself up. But you'll have to come and get me."

"It's me. Us. Andy. Are you okay?"

"Not very," came the faint reply. "I was trying to get into the tank when I lost my tailing, and I went straight in one side and then out the other and then I fell down this hole. It's horrible down here and I'm stuck and . . . ouch . . ."

The two listening in the attic heard a distant slithering sound, followed by the noise of rattling stones.

"I don't think I can hold on much longer," said Mervyn's voice, sounding even fainter than before.

"You *must!*" Andy ordered. "We'll get a rope. We'll be as quick as lightning."

"Hurry. . . ."

Andy edged backward across the tank and said fiercely to Ella, "Go and ask Aunt if she's got any rope. Say it's—it's for a game we're playing. And I'll see if Mr. Dunk's got one. Go on!"

Ella went like a dart from a blowpipe, with Andy thumping along behind her.

"Aunt!" Ella burst into the flat. "Have we got any . . . Aunt, what *are* you doing?"

Mrs. Tressida was standing on a small stool in the middle of the living-room floor with Lolly in her arms.

"Ella," said Mrs. Tressida in a rather wavering voice, "I don't want to worry you, my flower, but I think they're coming for me."

"Who are?" asked Ella, who was feeling quite distracted.

"The Sea People. I can sense them. I've been uneasy all night, but I put it down to fancy, but now I'm sure, though what deep game they're playing I don't understand. Young Neap up to his silly tricks again, I suppose. But they shan't have you as well. Pack your suitcase and get your ticket and . . ."

Mrs. Tressida stopped speaking abruptly and in the silence they could hear two things. The first was a rattling noise in the wall above the cupboard which was built into it, and the second was the familiar thump, thump, thump of Andy coming up the stairs. He came hurrying into the room with a great bundle of rope clutched in his arms, one end trailing behind him.

"I've got the clothesline," he said breathlessly. "Come on, Ella."

"Aunt says that the Sea People are coming."

"Andy, my flower, it's best that you—"

There was a tremendous rattling and bumping noise in the wall, a muffled howl, a thud, and then the door of the cupboard flew open and a cascade of rubble and dirt shot into the room, followed by an extremely dirty shape that rolled over and over until it came to rest in a silent heap right in front of Aunt. Nobody spoke for at least five seconds, and then Aunt said faintly, "Bless my stars, if it isn't a merboy. Well, he's nothing to worry about, poor little soul, he doesn't look as if he could harm a shrimp. I do believe he's knocked out cold too. Well, don't just stand there. Ella, go and get a flannel. Andy, fill a bowl with cold water. Well, stir yourselves, stir yourselves . . ."

They stirred.

Mervyn woke up about ten minutes later to find two anxious and one placid face watching him. His own face was an even paler shade of green than usual.

"I had to let go," he said. "I just couldn't hang on any longer. Oh, my tail!"

"You've twisted it," said Mrs. Tressida, "near enough a sprain it is. And you've bumped your head and skinned your hands and torn your weed sweater, but you'll live. Drink a drop of this and you'll feel more like it."

Mervyn did as he was told and slowly his skin became a more healthy shade of green. He was sitting propped up in the big armchair, with a towel around his shoulders and his tail in the bowl. He couldn't take his eyes off Aunt.

"There's a very strong fishy smell in here," she said, wrinkling up her little button nose.

And indeed there was. Lolly was walking around and around, with her whiskers twitching and her tail straight up. Suddenly she swerved toward Andy and began to claw at his coat.

"It's not me!" said Mervyn, sitting bolt upright, his green eyes starting to flash.

"It's me, I mean it's the haddock I saved from breakfast," Andy explained. "I kept it for you in case you were hungry, but I forgot all about it."

"Me—eat a *fish*?" said Mervyn in a horrified voice. "We Sea People aren't cannibals, you know."

Andy flushed a dull red and mumbled, "Well, I didn't know. How was I expected to know anyway?"

"Better give it to Lolly out in the kitchen," suggested Aunt. "Well, now, Mervyn, Ella, and Andy, you have told me just a few bits and pieces, and the rest I've put together for myself about what's been going on. In all my long life I've never heard the like. Young Neap won't care for it, you know. He'll get in one of his rages. Is he still as quick-tempered as ever he was?"

"He does get pretty cross at times," Mervyn agreed. "But I can't help it if he *does* rage. I'm not going back. I've been practicing land-living for ages and, although I still get a scratchy feeling in my skin when I've been out of water for a bit, I don't care. I'm staying."

"But you can't stay like that. I mean with a tail," Andy said, hoping that he wasn't going to ruffle Mervyn's feelings again.

"That's it," Mervyn said, leaning forward and gazing with bright green eyes at Aunt, who was watching placidly with her little gnarled hands folded in her lap. "You will help me, won't you? Ella told me you were a white witch, and I know about the trouble between you and Old Neap, so I shouldn't really be asking, but I don't know who else to ask."

"My flower, or perhaps I should say, my starfish, I'll do what I can, seeing as how you're so settled on it, but fish, skin, and bones, my magic isn't what it was. It's all over the place at the moment. I think it's all this machinery about these days that is doing it."

"Old Neap says the same. He goes dark green with rage when one of those big oil tankers comes overhead."

"Do you think he will try and get you back?" Ella asked anxiously.

"Oh, yes. There was an advance party out last night. I could hear them outside the Fort. That's why I got out of the bathtub, because I wanted to get as far into the middle of this place as I could."

"I'll tell you something else," said Andy, who had been investigating the back of the wall cupboard; "there was a little stairway up here once upon a time. It seems a funny sort of place to have it."

As he spoke there was the sound of a car drawing up outside and then two doors banged. Two voices spoke down in the courtyard, and Andy went over to the window and looked out. He could see the roof of a small van with a blue light on the top of it.

"It's the police," said Andy. "Well, at least *they* won't be looking for you, Mervyn. I wonder why they're here?"

"Then there is another problem," said Mrs. Tressida, who hadn't been paying much attention to all this. "And that is, even if I do manage to get rid of your tail, Mervyn, and make you some land legs, I don't see what can become of you afterward. You can't just suddenly appear on the island, you know. You'll have to live somewhere and go to school and . . . oh, my stars, now what?"

Feet thumped up the stone stairs, and just as the door opened with a crash, Andy snatched the towel from Mervyn's shoulders and threw it over his tail. Mr. Dunk burst into the room.

"Morning," he said to Mrs. Tressida, "sorry to bother you, but it's the police. They want to question you."

"Me? What about?"

"The prowler. While Mrs. Dunk was in town she reported that the Fort had been broken into. Well, nearly broken into. My word, that's a nasty mess you've got on the carpet there. Came down the chimney, I suppose. The chimneys need seeing to, as I told Mrs. Dunk, but then I can't be everywhere at once. I've got my hands more than full with this place, I can tell you. The police'll be up here in a moment. Thought I'd better let you know."

Mr. Dunk swung around, nearly collided with the door, and then hurled himself down the stone stairway.

Everybody sat, stood, or perched like statues for a moment, and then Mrs. Tressida said, "There's no point in trying to hide you, Mervyn, because Mr. Dunk's seen you. Andy, give him your duffel-coat and then tuck that towel right around his tail. Ella, help me sweep up all that rubble, and Lolly, for goodness' sake, my flower, get out of the way."

Everybody did as they were told as fast as they could and there was no time in which to ask questions, but even so, the last of the disguising of Mervyn and the sweeping up of the mess had only just been finished when footsteps were heard outside and Mr. Dunk announced loudly, "This way, officer. Mrs. Tressida and all, this is Officer Morgan."

Officer Morgan trod into the room with his notebook in his hand. He had quite a nice, not-very-young face, curly dark hair and bright brown eyes that, as far as Andy was concerned, looked as if they could see around corners. Mervyn's tail swished anxiously in the bowl underneath the towel, Ella gulped, and Lolly retreated to the kitchen to see if there was any fish left. Only Mrs. Tressida stayed perfectly still.

"Sorry to trouble you, madam," said Officer Morgan, "but I'm just making a few inquiries about this alleged prowler. Did you hear anything of an unusual nature last night?"

"I heard a great deal, but it wasn't unusual. Do sit down. What I heard was the sea getting up a bit. But then it often does at this time of year. But it was no more than that, so I can't help you, I'm afraid."

"Thank you, madam. Now, you'll be Andy?"

"Yes," croaked Andy. Out of the corner of one ear he could hear Mervyn's tail swishing and suddenly it seemed to be a terribly loud noise.

"Andy's staying with us," volunteered Mr. Dunk, "like I told you. If it wasn't for that bad leg of his he'd be able to help me with some of the repairs on this place. Slates, guttering, electrical work, central heating, let alone the TV and the phone, are always giving trouble. I can't keep up with it all single-handed, I really can't. And now with a prowler as well it's more than can be managed, as I've told Mrs. Dunk a hundred times."

"There certainly does seem to be a lot that needs doing," agreed Officer Morgan, suddenly becoming much less official for a moment, "I'm quite keen on do-it-yourself. Painting and decorating and all the rest of it."

"Oh, so am I," agreed Mr. Dunk. "Why, I'm working from morning till night."

Was it Andy's imagination, or did he for a fleeting second notice a twinkle in the policeman's bright brown eyes? The next moment he knew he hadn't because Officer Morgan was looking directly at him and saying, "Well, Andy, what about you? Did you see or hear anything suspicious?"

"No. Nothing," said Andy with his fingers crossed behind his back.

"H'm."

Because it was so gray and wintry outside, there was one lamp on in the living room, and Andy had the uneasy feeling that it was shining directly on him. Also, he was aware that several drops of water from the bowl had just appeared on the carpet near him. He didn't dare move to try and cover them, so he continued to stare back at the policeman, who now turned his attention to Ella.

"There's no need to be scared," he said. "You're Ella, aren't you? We're not at all sure that there was any prowler. It could have been a dog, or even a cow that had got away from her tether. It does happen. Have you got anything to report?"

Ella shook her head mutely.

And now the moment came that four people in the living

room had all realized at the same time was going to be very difficult, if not disastrous.

"And who have we here?" asked Officer Morgan, turning his attention to Mervyn.

"Mervyn," said Mervyn. "I'm a—"

"Friend of mine," said Andy.

"I don't think I know your face," said Morgan, leaning forward slightly. "You're very pale, lad. Been sick?"

There was just the slightest pause, and then Mrs. Tressida said calmly, "Yes, poor flower, he was climbing and missed his tail . . . his footing."

"I see. And where do you live, Mervyn?"

Officer Morgan moved slightly forward as he spoke, and both Andy and Ella had the extraordinary feeling that their hearts had moved upward and were now thudding away at the bottoms of their throats.

"The sea," said Mervyn, "I live—"

"He's a fisherman, or fisherboy, perhaps I should say," said Mrs. Tressida, "and you know how rough it was last night, Mr. Morgan. Poor soul, he hasn't quite recovered yet, which is another reason why he's so pale. But you'll feel better soon, won't you?"

"Oh, yes," agreed Mervyn, and just as he spoke and Officer Morgan took another step forward, the electric light went bright and then dark a couple of times and then went out.

"There," said Mr. Dunk in the half-light. "What did I tell you? Nothing but trouble. That'll be the main fuse blown. I never knew such a place. I wonder if you could give me a hand, Mr. Morgan? It's all too much for one man to deal with, it really is!"

CHAPTER X

Mistress Tree

10 Mistrees Tree

"HE'S SHARP, that one is," said Mrs. Tressida, when everybody's hearts had gotten back to their normal places. "And if *he* doesn't get you, Mervyn, the Sea People will, so bless me, we'll have to get a move on, and the sooner the better."

"But what can we do?" asked Ella, who was almost as pale as Mervyn. "Aunt, did you make the light go out like that?"

"I did, my flower, but only just. It was a struggle, I can truthfully tell you. The strange thing was . . . " and she looked over the top of her little round spectacles, " . . . it felt as if somebody else was giving me a helping hand, but we won't go into that now. *Now* all we can do is to keep Mervyn here overnight and to put out a little bit of magic around the

Fort, which should put the Sea People off the scent. The wind's died down, and that'll mean that Young Neap's gone quiet for a while. Whether that's good or bad, I can't say."

"It's very kind of you to help me," Mervyn said gruffly. "I know I shouldn't have asked, really."

"There, there. If we magic people don't help each other every once in a while, it's a poor lookout. And I'm too old and too homesick to quarrel about the rights and wrongs of it all. Young Neap's kept me imprisoned here all these years, so I know what it's like to be caught in a place where you don't want to be anymore. You just rest your tail while I see what can be done. Ella, I've got a job for you."

A little while later the lights all over the Fort came on suddenly and Andy, who was keeping watch by the window, saw Mr. Dunk and Officer Morgan come out of the front door. He could just hear Mr. Dunk saying, " . . . and if you'd care to give me a hand with the TV aerial, it would be a great help. I would do it myself, but it's my back that stops me from going up the ladder and . . ."

What Officer Morgan replied Andy couldn't catch, but he did see the policeman get into his van and drive off rather fast over the bumpy sand dunes. Mr. Dunk shook his head sadly and vanished inside the Fort. Then Ella appeared under the archway with a bulging plastic bag, which smelled very seaweedy when she came into the flat.

"Better put that on to simmer," said Mrs. Tressida, looking up from the thick old book she was reading, "that poor little merboy'll be starving by now. Which reminds me, it's our dinnertime, too. Andy, has that law man gone yet? Good, good. You go down and have your meal and I'll see you after. Oh dear, oh dear."

"Is anything the matter?"

"Yes, *me*! I'm old and out of practice and it wasn't till I started reading up on these spells that I realized just how much I've forgotten. Off with you, my flower."

Andy discovered yet again how being mixed up with magic and being scared half out of your skin can make a person ravenously hungry. Fortunately there was plenty of cauliflower and bacon and cheese omelet followed by stewed pears and custard.

"My word, you've got an appetite and a half, soldier," said Mr. Dunk admiringly as Andy passed up his plate for a third helping. "Nice chap, our policeman. He doesn't think there was any prowler. Says it was probably a cow got loose. I thought the same myself all along. But Mrs. Dunk was worried, and it's better to be safe than sorry. Are there any of those nice sweet biscuits left?"

"It does get dark so," said Mrs. Dunk, putting a large baking sheet on the table.

"Early. I know," said Andy, helping himself to a chocolate wafer.

"The TV's broken again. I'll have to see what I can do with it in a minute," said Mr. Dunk, sitting down heavily beside the stove, "and since I'll be so busy I wonder if you could take Tommy for a walk, Andy. Very fond of you he is."

"It would be," said Mrs. Dunk, rattling all the plates off the table and into the sink and turning on the tap so hard that a whole cloud of bubbles floated up all over the kitchen ceiling.

"All right," said Andy heavily, because he knew only too well how Tommy felt about Mervyn and there really had been troubles enough over the last twenty-four hours. "Come on, then, let me fasten your leash."

Tommy rolled his great brown eyes, bared his teeth, and dragged all four paws across the kitchen floor as Andy lugged him out of the Fort.

"Stupid dog," grumbled Andy as Tommy whined and tried to wrap himself around Andy's bad leg.

"Hello, beautiful," said Ella, bounding down the stone stairs and looking a lot less pale than she had the last time Andy had seen her. "Who's a beautiful dog then? Aunt says we're to draw chalk marks all around the Fort. She says it's white magic and she thinks it'll keep the Sea People off for about twenty-four hours, but she's not sure."

"You're in a good mood," said Andy suspiciously.

"Well, the policeman's gone and Mervyn's okay and anyway I rather like magic. Come on, we'd better hurry, because it'll be dark soon. Fish, skin, and bones, Mervyn's dinner smelled *awful*, but he seemed to like it. It was a kind of seaweed stew. Yuck. Now this is the sign we've got to draw. It's sort of like an arrowhead with a line through it. You take that side of the Fort and I'll do this one. Okay?"

Ella was in a very bossy mood and Andy wasn't at all sure that he didn't like it better when she was worried and anxious and depending on him. However, this was not the moment to mull over things like that, so he took the piece of chalk and, with Tommy hindering him every inch of the way, Andy began to draw the strange-looking signs on his side of the Fort until he and Ella met again at the far end.

By this time the sun was starting to set in a very pale way behind the sulky gray sea. The wind had died away completely, and the water had a kind of sullen look about it as it slowly rolled backward and forward with scarcely a ripple. Three dun-colored seagulls were floating slowly up and down, and a collection of oyster catchers were arguing and peering at each other on the water's edge as they picked their way in and out of the swags of dark seaweed. The beam from the mainland lighthouse flashed across the gathering darkness and far out on the horizon was what looked like a thick gray shawl lying on top of the water.

"Mist," said Ella, narrowing her eyes. "Aunt says they used to call it pirates' topcoats, but I don't know why. Come on, or you'll be late for tea."

"What about Mervyn?"

"Aunt says we're to meet at the little summerhouse right after lunch tomorrow. Isn't it *exciting?*"

"Mm," said Andy, who felt that he had had quite enough excitement to last him for a while.

The TV was now behaving itself perfectly, and it was nice just to sit in the warm kitchen with Mr. and Mrs. Dunk, who was darning socks at a tremendous rate. "It does seem a shame, because I'm sure she'd enjoy."

"Yes," agreed Mr. Dunk, who was chewing noisily on a toffee, "and she'll be lonely when young Ella goes back home at the end of the vacation. A nice old lady like her shouldn't be on her own. Mrs. Dunk and I have it in our minds that we should ask her if she'd like to move down with us."

"Oh, well, ah, er, I don't think . . ." said Andy, with horrible visions of the disasters that might befall the TV, the telephone, and the lights if this happened.

"Only we haven't really got the room," went on Mr.

Dunk. "Wind's dropped. I wonder if it'll rain tonight?"

"I hope not," said Andy fervently, because the rain would wash away the white magic signs on the Fort walls.

"You like it here on the island, don't?" asked Mrs. Dunk, looking more like a little mouse than ever as she bit through a piece of darning wool.

"Yes, I do, ever so much. It's . . . it's nice. I wish I lived here. I'm sure Mum'd like it too."

"If wishes were horses, then smugglers'd ride," said Mr. Dunk. "Here's the news."

Andy just about managed to keep his eyes open until the weather forecast. Fortunately rain was not on the map, although there were warnings of mist, followed by possible rising winds.

Andy meant to keep at least half an ear open for any possible invading Sea People, but within two minutes of getting into bed he was heavily asleep. In the morning he went off early to look for any signs of the Sea People in the sand dunes, but there was no sign of tailprints.

"Well done, Aunt," said Andy, and went to help Mr. Dunk, who was having trouble clearing up some of the broken guttering. Since Mr. Dunk's back was still bothering him quite a lot, Andy soon found himself doing most of the work.

"Very busy we've been," said Mr. Dunk over lunch. "All that bending hasn't done my back any good, I can tell you. I think I'd better rest it. You'll take Tommy for a little walk, won't you, soldier?"

Tommy was still in an uneasy, whining mood as Andy lugged him up the narrow, brambly path toward the little summerhouse. He had been wondering how Aunt would be able to get Mervyn up the hillside, but when he turned the corner he saw that an old baby carriage was parked to one side underneath the blackberry bushes.

"Aunt and I got him up between us," said Ella, "and do you know, Mervyn only spent half the night in the bathtub and Aunt says that proves he's almost a land person."

"Hello, Andy, my flower," said Mrs. Tressida, putting her head around the door. "My stars, it was hard work getting Mervyn up here. I'm getting too old for all of this, and that's a fact. Well, come inside. Nice little place, isn't it? I always did like it up here on the hill long before this place was built. Now then, Mervyn, sit down on that side of the bed. Tommy, lie down and behave yourself. Stop it, I say!"

Tommy, whose eyes were rolling horribly, tried to launch himself at Mervyn, who shrank back, which was not surprising since Tommy had started to snap and snarl.

"There, now," said Mrs. Tressida, "Sea People and land creatures never have seen eye to eye since that silly meeting when Young Neap began to throw his weight about. You'll have to take him outside, Andy, and for goodness' sake see he's tied up properly."

Luckily Andy was able to find a strong root in the bracken. He looped the leash around it and then went back into the summerhouse. Although it was only early afternoon the sea mist was making everything rather gray and indistinct.

"Well, now," said Mrs. Tressida, rolling up her sleeves in a businesslike manner, "I'm not at all sure that this is going to work properly, but it's the best I can do. Are you ready, Mervyn Sea Person?"

"Ready," said Mervyn, who was looking distinctly green.

"Right, then. All join hands and look toward me," ordered Mrs. Tressida.

Everybody did as they were told and after a moment or so the murky gray light from outside began to fade away and a clear green-white light started to grow and glow in front of their eyes. It seemed to shimmer backward and forward until nobody could bear to look at it a moment longer. At the same time Andy could hear a faint thin voice calling or singing, only he couldn't quite catch what it was saying, no matter how much he strained his ears.

"Oh, oh, oh, my fins and tails," somebody said in a whisper.

And then a second voice. "Drat! It's gone wrong!"

Very slowly Andy opened his eyes and for a moment he was quite dazzled by the brightness, but this time it was a golden-yellow light that made him blind, and, even more surprising, it was decidedly warm.

"Andy," said Ella's voice, "what's happened?"

Andy and Ella and Mervyn, still holding hands, were sitting in a circle exactly as they had been only a minute ago. Only now, instead of having a tail, Mervyn had two legs sticking out from underneath an old raincoat of Ella's that he was wearing. They were perfectly good ordinary legs that ended in feet, with only one small thing wrong with them. They were pale green.

Several other things had changed too. The little summerhouse in which they had been sitting had vanished, the sun was still fairly high in the sky, the sea was blue instead of gray, and there was no sign of Aunt. Where she should have been was a small lady in a long gray cloak.

"Well, then," said the stranger, "here's a surprise!"

Andy, Ella, and Mervyn couldn't think of a word between them, because whatever had happened had happened too fast for them to get their breaths back.

"Cat got your tongues?" asked the lady, sinking down onto her knees so that her cloak billowed around her feet. "You've got pale-green legs and feet, my flower. That's no good."

"Um, um, um," said Mervyn in a mumble. Then he took a deep breath and shouted, "I don't care *what* color they are! I've got legs and feet! *I've got legs and feet!*"

And Mervyn shook off the hands of Andy and Ella and got up and began to walk backward and forward with his knees bent. It was rather a staggering walk, but he refused to let anybody help him. At last he sank down on his knees in an exhausted heap.

While all this was going on, Ella had been sitting quietly with her chin on her knees, gazing steadily at the strange lady. Andy, of course, had taken the opportunity to do some looking around.

Down below them the Fort had changed very little, although the slit windows had been replaced by slightly larger openings and a fat chimney had been built on. Surrounding the Fort was a whole collection of small wooden buildings, with what looked like grass roofs kept in place by a crosscross of tarred ropes. The road was in a rather poor condition with broken paving stones, a number of which were missing, and with tufts of grass growing in the empty patches. There was still quite a lot of the R. XII to be seen, parts of it sticking out in jagged lumps far out into the sparkling sea.

There were also a number of small houses built around the edge of the bay. They were made partly of wood and partly of blocks and boulders, and it was all too obvious where a great deal of the old Roman road had gone. It had turned into walls. Directly below was a rickety-looking little wooden jetty, with several roughly made boats tied up to it. There were still a number of goats around, but their horns were shorter, and so were their rough coats. And dotted in among them were a number of cows, who were munching contentedly at the coarse grass.

Altogether it was a rather pretty scene, and it was also a great deal more peaceful than it had been the last time they had traveled backward. The only thing was, how *far* had they gone?

Andy turned his attention to the lady, who was now making a daisy chain. Ella was staring at her with a fixed frown and Mervyn was doing jogging on-the-spot exercises.

"You'll know me again," the lady said, finishing the chain off neatly and putting it over Ella's head. "My name's Mistress Tree and I live in the Fort down below there. And who might you be?"

They told her and Andy added, "Mervyn is a Sea Person. Or at least he *was*. But you knew that, didn't you?"

"Sharp," said the lady, "you're not as blue as you're blackberry looking. I know a lot of things. It's my business. And there's not too many green legs and feet about these days. Exercise your toes, my flower, they'll be weak and poorly for a bit yet."

"Toes!" said Mervyn ecstatically, and did as she suggested.

Mistress Tree had such a calm, gentle face that Andy decided he could trust her.

"Weren't you surprised to see us suddenly appear like that?" he asked.

"I was and I wasn't," Mistress Tree chuckled as though something were amusing her. "*You'd* be the one who'd be surprised if you knew how many people just appear on this island and then vanish again, like a puff of smoke overnight. It's going on all the time."

"What—what time is this?"

"Autumn. We go by seasons on the island; we don't take much account of years."

"I like it here," announced Mervyn, rolling over and over and kicking his green feet in the air. "Do people come and ask other people a lot of questions like they do in other places?"

"No, we don't ask too many questions. It isn't considered good manners on the island. Truth to tell," and she smiled, "we've all got too much to hide and that's the top and toe of it."

"But somebody's going to say something about Mervyn's green legs, surely?" Andy persisted. He could just imagine what a stir they would have created in his own time. "They" would probably have whizzed him off to the hospital and given him injections and tests, and there would have been stories about Mervyn in the newspapers and on the TV, and there would be thousands and thousands of questions. Andy shuddered at the thought.

"It could be spread around that he's from some far island over the seas and that all the people there have green legs.

Besides which, the green'll go in time, and so will that pale face of his, and then he'll be as brown as all the other island people."

Although he had been told in the nicest possible way that it wasn't polite to ask questions, Andy couldn't help going on.

"Supposing... just supposing that the Sea People thought that because he's got green legs he should really go and live with them? They might come and capture him in the dead of night."

"But he isn't a Sea Person, my flower. He's just another boy. They'd have no rights to him, so they'd leave him be. It's no skin off their scales."

"*Can* I stay?" Mervyn asked anxiously.

"We'll see. I must say we could do with some more help around the Fort, with the chickens and geese as well as the cows and goats. Then there's always a bit of repairing to be done. I've got old Dunker, who is supposed to do odd jobs, but he spends most of his time ... well, doing other things. Would you like to come down and have a look around the Fort? It's an interesting old place."

Andy and Ella looked at each other. It would be fun to explore, but on the other hand ...

"We've got to get back to where we belong by suppertime," Ella said.

"That's no problem. We'll just take a tuck in time, as the saying goes, so that you'll have hardly been away at all."

Mistress Tree got to her feet and shook out her full skirts.

"Mind you, I have to say that it isn't always as peaceful as this. Sometimes it's amazingly lively."

"Raiders?" Ella asked anxiously.

"Of a kind. But it's not the season for them. Well?"

It took Andy and Ella about two seconds to make up their minds.

"We'll stay," Andy said, "but only till suppertime."

As for Mervyn, he was already halfway down the hill.

CHAPTER XI

Pirates and
Smugglers

Inside, the Fort had changed quite a lot since the Romans
had built it for a garrison. Most of the ground floor was a
large kitchen and living place, with heavy wooden tables,
benches, and stools. There was a big fireplace with a thick
iron bar hung over it, and a stone oven to one side, from
which came the most marvelous smell of baking bread. The
far end was like one large storeroom, piled high with bulging, coarse sacks of provisions from flour to onions, dried
fish (which upset Mervyn a little) to sweet-smelling apples
and carrots. There were also several mounds of potatoes.

"I say," Andy exclaimed, his eyes round with respect, "is
this all *your* food, Mistress Tree?"

"Goodness me, no. This is the storehouse for the whole

island. Every islander brings the crops that he grows here and then we share and share alike. Perhaps one'll grow nothing but potatoes, while another is a fisherman. Well, you'd get sick to death of eating just what you'd either grown or caught, wouldn't you? But this way everybody gets a good mixture."

"I wonder why *we* don't do it?" said Andy, who was busy sniffing his way around. He absolutely hated going to the giant supermarket on Saturdays with his mother, because it was always crowded with people pushing and shoving and banging into one another with their sharp metal shopping carts.

"Just look at the eggs!" said Ella. "They're ginormous!"

"Duck eggs to the left, goose in the middle, hens to the right," said Mistress Tree, taking off her cloak and then flapping it at a couple of hens and a duck who had come clucking and quacking through the open door and were now happily rooting around underneath the benches. "Where can Dunker have got to? Gone fishing again, I suppose!"

"What's upstairs?" asked Mervyn, who wanted to get away from the subject of fish.

"Go and explore," said Mistress Tree, tying a large apron around her waist and hanging a big iron pot from a hook that was fixed over the fireplace.

They clattered up the wooden staircase and on the next floor any resemblance to the Fort they knew and the one in which they now found themselves ended. There was a whole maze of little rooms, which were very sparsely furnished and had dark, unpainted wooden walls.

"This must be our living room, I think," Ella said uncertainly, "but where's the bathroom gone to?"

"There aren't any bathrooms," said Andy. "What a great idea. Hang on. Yes, this part's your living room, because there's that built-in cupboard thing that Mervyn fell out of. Only now it looks quite new. Hey, look at this."

Andy opened the cupboard door and, with some difficulty because of his leg, managed to half-climb inside it. It was more shallow then he remembered and then he realized why: There was another door at the back that slid sideways and beyond that was a tiny, curving staircase leading upward.

"Hey, Mervyn, are you up there?" Andy shouted.

"Yes," Mervyn's voice came back faintly down the stairway. "I'm in the place where the tank was. At least, I think I am. Come up."

"Can't," said Andy regretfully. "Here, Ella, you have a try."

Ella obligingly squirmed her way upward and arrived rather dirty and dusty on the top floor where Mervyn was wiggling his toes and doing a kind of knee-bend exercise as he talked.

"Look," he said, helping Ella out of the tiny doorway in the wall, "there's a little window here and you can see right out over the bay, sort of sideways on."

There was no glass in the window and the pair of them peered out across the rippling blue-purple water. The short autumn evening was nearly over and a thin line of mist was sliding in across the sea as the sun settled down in a great crimson ball and the first stars began to twinkle in the blue sky.

"That star's very low," Ella said, pointing with one dusty finger.

Mervyn's emerald-green eyes were still those of a Sea Person, which meant that he could see farther and more sharply than Ella could.

"That's not a star," he said, "it's a ship. The sun's reflecting off something on her mast. She's got a strange sort of flag."

"Strange?" said Ella in a hollow voice.

"Yes. It's a skull with two bones crossed behind it. I remember Old Neap telling us about flags like that. They're used by . . . by . . ,"

"Pirates," whispered Ella. "Are they coming this way?"

"No, she's anchored to the right of the Gannet Rocks. She's out of sight from the shore. Hey, Ella, where are you going?"

But Ella was already going full tilt down the tiny stairway, shouting as she went. "Andy, quick, there's a pirate ship. ANDY!"

What happened during the next half hour was a kind of blur. One moment there seemed to be only the four of them in the Fort, and the next there were people running in all directions.

"Dratted pirates," muttered Mistress Tree, taking the soup off the boil, "why can't they leave us alone, then! It's the stores they're after and a bit more besides, I shouldn't wonder. Mervyn, you've got the best eyes of all of us, so you stay by that window and keep watch. Ella, you go with him and the second he reports any movement you come down that stairway on the double. All the way down, that is, till you reach here."

Mistress Tree pushed at part of the wall to the left of the fireplace and the big stone block slid sideways to reveal a small cavity.

"But that's where the Romans kept their wages," Andy said.

"Very likely. And that's where one or two other treasures have been kept in their own rightful time, and don't you forget that. Andy, you go and call in the chickens with this little pipe. Just give it a good hard blow."

"But why bother about them now?"

"Don't ask any more questions. Just blow as hard as your lungs'll allow. Now, hurry. Dratted pirates, coming early like this!"

Feeling a bit silly, Andy thumped out into the courtyard of the Fort, took a deep breath, and blew. The pipe produced a surprisingly loud, shrill note and chickens started appearing from all over the place.

The sun had set by now and up above the stars were starting to shine quite brightly, and it was only lower down toward the horizon that everything was muted by the rolling sea mist.

"Once again, soldier," ordered Mistress Tree, pulling on her cloak. Andy did as he was told and this time the shrill call was answered by the sound of running footsteps, the first of which belonged to a small man with a beaky nose and bright-blue eyes.

"Came as fast as I could," he said breathlessly. "Been fishing. Hello, you're new here, aren't you? Dunker's my name. Well, I need a nice sit-down for a moment or two, that's certain."

And he settled himself on the nearest stool and stretched out his legs toward the fire as he went on: "There's never a moment's peace in this place. I'm on the go from morning till night, what with one thing and another. And there was me and my friend just having a little bit of time off when you go and sound the alarm. It's all too much and so I tell you. Here he comes now."

Another breathless figure, slightly larger than that of Mr. Dunker, came hurrying into the Fort. He had curling dark hair and very sharp brown eyes, which seemed to be looking in all directions at once.

"Now what?" he asked. "I was laying out lobster pots and don't let anybody say different!"

"You were up to your usual tricks, Jem Morgan," said Mistress Tree calmly. "A smuggler you were almost born and a smuggler you will end. But that's neither here nor the other place at the moment. You and your uncle, whom I well remember, are as like as two peas that ever came out of the same pod."

"Well, my uncle is one of the most respected of the fraternity. There's no one that can touch him, so they say. Sir Harry, they call him out in the Western Indies Isles. Well, then, what's going on?'"

"There's a skull and crossbones anchored offshore. They'll be after our stores, my flower. And since there'll be a large number of them, and few of us, we must raise as many islanders as we can. There's lookouts posted at the spy window."

"And this wounded soldier here?"

"One of us," Mistress Tree said crisply. "He's come to

the rescue before and will do again, I daresay. It was his
friends Mervyn and Ella who saw the ship in the first place.
You can get Andy, here, to give you a hand."

Andy, who had been watching and listening as hard as he
could, now found himself being hauled out of the Fort just
as a whole crowd of islanders surged into it. He wasn't at all
sure what exactly was going on, but at the back of his mind
he was at least certain of one thing. And that was that the
sooner he and Ella got back to their own time, the better it
would be for the pair of them. And then he remembered
Mervyn. They couldn't just leave him to face the pirates.

"Darn!" said Andy furiously.

"My sentiments entirely," agreed Jem Morgan, hitching
up his greasy sheepskin jacket. "Well, if Mistress Tree
gives you a good name, then that's all right by me. Off we go
then, to beat those pirates at their own game. Before they
get a chance to wreck us, *we* wreck *them*, agreed?"

"How?"

"I'll show you. There's nothing like learning a trade if you
want to make your way in life, and a good smuggler never
goes hungry. Now just you grab hold of that donkey."

The donkey, a beautiful creature with large, calm eyes
and delicate little hooves, was munching quietly at the
grass growing between the broken flagstones of the Roman
road. She had a rope halter around her neck and didn't
seem to mind Andy's coming up to her and taking hold of it.
She nuzzled at his hand, which he wasn't too keen on, since
she had very large teeth.

"Bless you, she won't hurt. Best little smuggler on the
island, is Nell," said Jem, coming out of one of the stables
with a large lantern in one hand, a length of rope in the

other, and a bulky leather saddle under one arm.

He stood for a moment in the starlight, considering Andy with his head on one side.

"With that bad leg of yours you won't be able to follow the path, so you'd best ride. Up you get."

"You mean ride on Nell?" Andy asked a shade nervously. He'd never ridden anything except a wooden merry-go-round horse at a fair.

"Well, *I'm* not carrying you. Move, soldier."

Nell stood like a rock as Andy, standing on his good leg, cautiously hitched his bad leg over her back and then humped himself into position. Since Nell wasn't very big his feet nearly touched the ground. He soon discovered that riding a donkey bareback was not exactly comfortable—Nell turned out to be surpringly bony.

"That's the way," Jem said. "All right, Nell, you know the path . . . off you go."

The mist was swirling in off the sea by now, eddying and billowing across the dunes and somehow making the whole situation more and more unreal every moment, as Nell began to pick her way up the dark hillside, with Jem trudging along behind.

"They," Jem said, "won't know we've spotted them yet, seeing as how they've anchored around the point. The only place from which they could've been spotted was through the—ahem—smugglers' window. They'll stay out there until the mist's really thick and then they'll come sailing into the harbor as bold as the brass earrings they wear, hoping to catch us unawares."

"What . . . what happens then?"

"Oh, the usual. They'll raid the Fort and take all our

winter food supplies *and* anything else they fancy. Then they'll try to set fire to the place, which is nothing but silly spite, and then off they'll go again. They're early this season. They don't usually try their tricks until the real sea fogs set in, and then we'd have had a lookout up in the window. Fortunate, it was, that your friends were there."

"Who . . . who usually wins?"

"Sometimes it's us. Sometimes it's them, depending on who gets caught napping, you might say. But for myself I call it cheating to come a month early. It's not playing by the rules, is it, soldier?"

"I suppose not," replied Andy, who in spite of feeling distinctly nervous, also felt that he could be listening to someone talking about a rival soccer club that had decided to do some early training.

"Smugglers versus pirates," Andy muttered, and then added "Ouch!" as Nell scrambled over some boulders.

"Nearly there," grunted Jem.

They were quite high up now, and it really was an extraordinary sight looking down on the bay, which was shrouded in the rolling mist so that only the roof of the Fort was showing.

"Now comes the difficult part," said Jem. "Down you go, Nell; hang on tight, soldier."

He spoke just in time, for one moment Nell's long ears were ahead of Andy and the next they vanished as she put down her head and somehow, without losing her footing, managed to go right over the top of the hillside. Andy sat back as far as he could, his legs stuck straight out in front of him. There seemed to be nothing between him and a sheer drop down to the sea. It was a nightmarish descent, and just as Andy thought it would never stop, and that at any minute he would go clean over both Nell's head and the cliff, her little hooves came to a neat halt.

"Scarifying, isn't it?" said Jem breathlessly. "Well done, Nell. Off you get, soldier."

Only too glad to do what he was told for once, Andy slid off Nell's back and sat down cautiously on the nearest boulder.

"Now we wait," said Jem, "until Dunker lights his lanterns. Peaceful, isn't it?"

"Er," agreed Andy, rubbing his aching seat. "I'm sorry, but I still don't understand what's happening."

"Oh, it's simple enough. Here, give me a hand with fixing this saddle and making it secure."

It was a strange-shaped saddle with two prongs at either end. Once it was in position Jem picked up the heavy lantern and fitted it snugly onto the saddle, and then made it fast to the prongs with a length of twine.

"Now the rope," Jem said. "You take one end and I take the other and we wind it in and out of Nell's legs in a proper old cat's cradle."

"Simple enough?" asked Andy, when this curious business was finished.

"Simple as falling off a cliff. The pirates are anchored off the Gannet Rocks, right? As soon as they think it's time they'll up anchor and come sailing into the bay. They don't know that *we* know they're here. So, as is our nice, peaceful, friendly custom, we'll set out our harbor lights to left and right of the bay. *But*, soldier, the lights we are *really* going to set out will be in a different sort of a place than where they *should* be. And just to make it look bang to rights, there's this little boat floating up and down to the right of that nice, safe harbor, putting out her lobster pots as like as not. Got me?"

"I'm beginning to think so," Andy said slowly. "You mean Nell's going to be that boat. But I still don't understand how you can turn a donkey into a boat!"

"You will, you will. Now settle back and wait. . . . "

CHAPTER XII

The Wreckers

ANDY MUST HAVE DOZED off in spite of his aching seat, because one moment he was worrying about the big damp patch in the kitchen ceiling and telling his mother that the Horrible Landlord was a pirate, and the next he was sitting bolt upright with Jem's voice buzzing in his ear.

"Here we go, then. There's the harbor lights."

Two beacons blazed up to their left. They were rather blurred because of the mist, but still they shone with surprising brightness in the darkness.

"And here comes our nice little boat at anchor," said Jem. There was a rasping sound, a spark, and then the lantern on Nell's back began to send out a gold beam.

"Help me lead her," Jem said.

Gently but firmly led by her rope halter, Nell started to walk forward across the crunching shingle, but because of the ropes around her legs she moved in a rocking motion, up and down, up and down, and Andy, sheltering his eyes from the light, saw that it was exactly like looking at a little boat bobbing at anchor. And then, listening intently, they could hear the growl of the outgoing tide as it swirled around the rocks only a few feet away. For what seemed a very long time nothing happened, and then slowly and majestically a dark shape appeared out of the darkness.

"It's her," Andy and Jem said together.

"She's taken the bait," Jem whispered, "she's coming straight in."

There was something awe-inspiring and terrible about the slow, stealthy approach of the pirate ship as she silently billowed into the trap that had been laid for her. Up and down rocked Nell, the mist curling around her, at one moment blotting out her glowing lantern and then clearing away again so that the light shone steadily. And all the time there was the deep growl of the sea as it swirled around the rocks.

"Come on, my beauty, come on," whispered Jem, his eyes glittering. "This'll teach you not to stick to the rules."

"Yes, but what about the men on board?" asked Andy, because suddenly everything had stopped being dreamlike and had become horribly real.

"Some'll come ashore and some won't, I daresay. Well, that's the way it goes. And there'll be a lot of pirate treasure on board, too, which'll be rich pickings for the island."

"But . . . " said Andy and at the same moment there was a

great crunching noise. In the starlight he could see that the pirate ship had started to swivel around, its dark sails beginning to flutter helplessly; and above the sound of the sea he could hear voices calling and shouting.

"She's on the rocks," said Jem; "she'll be holed below the waterline and she's done for. It'll mean the island'll be free all winter! Give us your hand, soldier. You've done us a real good turn, you and those friends of yours. Turn off the lantern and help me undo Nell."

By the time they reached the Fort, nearly all the excitement was over. Everybody was talking at once as they gave their version of what had been happening and several damp and very downhearted-looking pirates were sitting on the oak benches with steam rising out of their clothes.

"They're not so green as they're cabbage-looking," said Mistress Tree, who was dolloping out great bowls of soup.

"Was anybody drowned?" asked Andy, who felt as if he were aching in every bone and muscle.

"Not a one, my flower. It's low tide, do you see, so that when their ship was holed on Gannet Reef below the rocks and taking on water fast, they jumped for it. Into five feet of slack water!"

"Don't go on about it, mussus," said one of the pirates, holding out an earthenware bowl. "Can I have some more of that gruel? Thanks. Mind you, next time we won't get caught by the same old tricks."

"It was ever so exciting," said Ella, slithering to a halt by Andy. "Mervyn and I were keeping watch up in that little window. And then Mr. Dunker shouted up, was it time to light the beacons? I couldn't see anything, but—"

"I could," said Mervyn, whose eyes were like green

stars, and who was almost pink-looking with triumph, "so I shouted down her distances and then the beacons were fired and we saw you light over to the right and I ran down the stairs and—"

"Fell down them, more like," said Mr. Dunker, cleaning his soup bowl with a hunk of dark-brown bread. "There was a rumbling and a rattling and the next thing was that this green shrimp here shot out of, er, thin air, as you might say. Any more of that soup left? It's hungry work, wrecking."

"He doesn't want the pirates to know about you-know-what," said Mervyn in a low voice, jerking his head to where the secret staircase came out in the kitchen. Only now, of course, the stone door was back in position so that nobody could guess that it was there at all. "They're going to take some of the pirate treasure off the ship at first light and store it in there. It's great having feet, but they do ache a bit."

And Mervyn stretched out his legs, which were now encased in some leather trousers that Mistress Tree had given him. His green and very dirty feet stuck out at the end of them.

"Here, you'd better have your coat back, thanks for the loan," Mervyn went on, shrugging himself out of Ella's raincoat. He had also acquired from the smugglers' considerable hoard a rough shirt and a leather jerkin.

Ella said slowly, "Thanks. You know, you look as if you belong here now. As if it's the right time for you."

"I'd *like* to stay, if they'll have me."

"You won't mind about pirates and smugglers and wrecking?" asked Andy.

"No, I *like* it."

"Let you stay? 'Course we will," said Jem, coming up and giving him a slap on the shoulder. "You're one of us now, and we can use those eyes of yours. They'll be what we might call our secret weapon. Very useful. You'll make a fine smuggler one of these days, or my name's not Jem Morgan."

Mervyn looked positively dazzled at this marvelous prospect and was quite unable to speak for a moment or two. He was still only just beginning to grasp that not only had he legs, but that he was also free of Old Neap for good and always. A great deal had happened to him in a very short space of time, and suddenly he felt so exhausted he could hardly move.

"Bed," said Mistress Tree, "here's a blanket and a bowl of water in case you start feeling scratchy in the middle of the night. You're sure to get attacks of it from time to time yet awhile. You can have the small room at the top of the stairs."

Mervyn got rather shakily to his green feet and he and Andy and Ella looked at each other for a moment. There was so much to say that not even Andy could think of a word until Mervyn said gruffly, "Well, thanks. Thanks very much. I hope we'll meet again one day."

He ducked his shaggy dark head, looked at them for a moment longer with his glittering emerald eyes, and then turned away and began to climb the stairs. Their last view of him was of two very dusty, pale-green feet vanishing into the darkness.

"We'd better get back," Andy said quickly, because Ella was starting to look upset. "But before we do, can I ask just one more question, Mistress Tree?"

"It's a good thing *you're* not staying," she said, smoothing out her gray cloak. "Well?"

"What'll happen to the pirates?"

"I shouldn't be surprised if some of them decide to stay. It's happened before and it'll happen again. Look at Jem, for one; he comes from one of the very *best* pirate families. He's got uncles and cousins and nephews flying the skull and crossbones all over the globe. He only turned to smuggling a few seasons ago after *he* was wrecked."

Jem was now deep in conversation with the captain of the pirate ship, a square-faced man who was just lighting a clay pipe and, as the light from his taper plopped up and down, Andy had the distinct feeling that he'd seen the man somewhere before. It was something to do with boats and fishing . . . but he couldn't pinpoint where or when it was they could possibly have met.

"Don't fret your head about it," Mistress Tree said in his ear. "It'll all come clear one day. Magic goes in circles, just like time does, my flower. The captain's one of them that'll stay here for good and all. As for the rest, we'll put 'em to work and those that want to settle will, the others'll get itchy feet and they'll build themselves a new ship from the wreck of the old one, and one fine, dark night they'll be off, and in a season or three they'll come sailing in as bold as the brass earrings they wear and it'll be us against them, same as always. But with Mervyn on *our* side, the dice'll be loaded in our favor, I shouldn't wonder. Now, that's enough. Come along with me."

Andy and Ella stood in the doorway for a moment, their eyes smarting from the smoke that was billowing out from the fireplace. Pirates and smugglers were now all talking together, with mugs of ale in their hands, and snatches of conversation reached the trio in the doorway.

" . . . not right to come a month early. Not playing by the rules . . . "

" . . . nearly caught you napping this time . . . "

" . . . always fancied settling down and growing potatoes . . . "

" . . . no, no, Sir Harry Morgan's my *uncle*. They do say he's got a fair old treasure buried out in those Western Indies Isles. Of course, since I've turned smuggler I'm not interested in *long* voyages . . . "

" . . . a very remarkable pirate. Right at the top of the tree. Tell me, Jem, who owns this Fort? I've taken a real fancy to it . . . "

" . . . tired out. It's all very well for you, sailing about in a big boat with nothing to do all day, but I can tell you it's too much work looking after a big place like this and . . . "

The door closed gently, and, in the sudden darkness, neither Andy nor Ella could see anything for a moment. And then, as they stood blinking and rather bewildered, the soft voice of Mistress Tree said, "Time to be gone, join hands and away you go."

The blanketing dark turned green and the mist swirled up and over their heads and the rumbling voices from inside the Fort faded away, to be replaced by the booming of the sea. Suddenly it wasn't warm anymore, but distinctly chilly, and something was wrapping itself around and around Andy's bad leg.

"Get off," Andy said.

"Aaaar," said Tommy, leaping up and down trying to lick Andy's ears. It wasn't quite as dark as it had been a minute ago, and they could see that they were standing in the overgrown courtyard of the Fort. There was no sign of Mistress Tree.

"Well, that's that then," Andy said, "but how did she know about Mervyn feeling itchy when he's away from water for a bit?"

"But don't you see?" replied Ella, following this line of thought easily. "She is—was, rather—a witch. And what's more—"

A dazzling light suddenly shone in their eyes and, for a second, they both wondered if a beacon had been lighted; and then the door into the Fort was flung open and Mr. Dunk appeared.

"There you are," he said, "Mrs. Dunk and me were just starting to get worried about you. The wind's getting up and no mistake. That'll bring a few more slates off the roof, I shouldn't be surprised. *And* the TV's playing up. Mrs. Dunk and me have quite decided that it's more than time we left the island and settled on the mainland. Which we would do tomorrow, if only we had the money."

Something that Mistress Tree had said drifted through Andy's mind. Something about not forgetting. . . . But not forgetting *what*?

"And another thing," said Mr. Dunk, tripping over a loose paving stone, "your ma's been trying to call you, Andy. Sounded rather upset, she did because of some sort of trouble with a ceiling coming down. Well, look lively, lad. Don't just stand there with your mouth open."

"Coming," said Andy, trying to unwind himself from Tommy's leash. "See you tomorrow, Ella."

Slowly Ella made her way up the stone staircase and into

the apartment, where Aunt, looking very tired, was dozing in front of the fire.

"Aunt," said Ella, crouching down on the floor and picking up Lolly, "Aunt, there's something I'd like to ask you."

"Ask away, my flower."

"Well," Ella said, "it's about Tress and Mistress Tree and *you*!"

CHAPTER XIII

Old Neap and the Wounded Knight

MR. DUNK was quite right about one thing, the wind *was* getting up and continued to do so during the next forty-eight hours. The sea and the sky were a deep gray and the waves came racing in from the horizon and hurled them-selves at the island, sending up great clouds of hissing spray. Everything seemed to be covered in a salty mist. Down by the harbor the sea picked up big boulders and used them to pound at the wall, so that there was a booming noise going on all the time. Pieces of the causeway and the Roman paving stones down by the bay were heaved away, and what had once been the R.XII became more of a ruin than ever.

All the fishing boats were hauled ashore, along with the

private craft, and the islanders fastened their storm windows and huddled in front of their fires and their TV sets and waited for the storm to blow itself out.

"Would you like to come down to the harbor with me?" asked Officer Morgan, driving up in his police van with the blue light going around and around on the roof.

"No, thank you, it's too" said Mrs. Dunk.

"Rough," agreed Mr. Dunk, "and I'd better stay here, seeing as how the slates are coming off the roof a dozen a minute or thereabouts."

"They need nailing down," said Officer Morgan. "It's a fine old roof, and it's a shame to see it going to waste. When I've got my day off maybe I'll come around and give you a hand. That TV aerial doesn't look any too safe either."

"Yes, the picture's been dreadful again," said Mr. Dunk, settling down in front of the stove. "We could hardly follow the cowboy film last night. Mind you, on the mainland we wouldn't have these difficulties. Perhaps Andy and Ella'd like to go with you."

It was very exciting and a bit scary to drive across the island with the wind tearing at the van as though at any minute it were going to blow it clean off the road.

"I've got a lot to tell you about Aunt," said Ella in a low voice as they bounced up and down on the back seat. "She says the storm's been blown up by Old Neap because he's in such a temper about losing Mervyn. And, what's more . . ."

"I've got a lot to tell you about my mum," cut in Andy. "The ceiling's come down in our kitchen, but the Horrible Landlord is raising the rent just the same, so we've got to find somewhere else to live. And, although she doesn't say anything about it, I think she's jolly sick of working in that rotten old cafeteria. She likes cooking for just a few people."

"Good cook, is she?" asked Officer Morgan over his shoulder.

"Terrific," said Andy, "even better than Mrs. Dunk. Wow, that was a big wave!"

"The seventh wave that would be. That's always the biggest one, they say. Well, why doesn't your ma do a swap with Mrs. Dunk then? The Dunks are dead set on leaving the island, if they can find the way to do it, and then the Fort'll need a new caretaker. Of course, your ma wouldn't be able to do all the repairs and upkeep that are needed, but I daresay I could do some of it. Here comes another seventh. . . ."

"You mean us live on the island!" said Andy. It was like a dazzling bright light shining in his eyes.

"It's just an idea," said Officer Morgan. "Here comes a real whopper."

"About Aunt," said Ella, "oh!"

The wave came curling in like a glassy green mountain range on the move, and although it was at least a hundred yards away, everybody ducked instinctively and at the same time the radio crackled and a rather distorted voice said, " . . . tanker in trouble and shifting her load . . . "

"That's all we need," said Officer Morgan. "If it really *does* shift, there could be oil coming ashore on the next high tide. So I'd best get the pair of you back to the Fort."

The wind backed off slightly during the night, but when everybody woke up the following morning there was a simply awful smell hanging over everything, and, as though drawn by a magnet, Mr. and Mrs. Dunk, Aunt, Ella, Andy, Officer Morgan, and Mr. Remuson all arrived at the beach at the same time. It was ringed in an evil-smelling gray-green sludge. Two oyster catchers, a sea gull, and a shag, their feathers coated with oil, were flapping helplessly on the sand. Everybody started talking at once, so that there was a babble of voices and then, quite suddenly, everything seemed to go click-click-click in Andy's mind.

He thumped his way across the sand, feeling braver than he had ever in his whole life, because he knew that although he was only Andy Jones, he was also in some extraordinary way the "wounded knight" who had to come to the rescue.

"Aunt," he said, planting himself fair and square in front of her.

"Yes, my flower," she said quietly as she rested her gnarled little hands on her walking stick.

"It's the island being attacked all over again, isn't it? First it was the North Sea men and then the pirates and now it's the oil. But the oil kills everything. The birds and their eggs and nests. All the small creatures that live along the beach *and* the creatures that live in the sea. So that makes it the enemy of the Land People *and* the Sea People. And that means,"— Andy took a deep breath—"if you're going to beat it, you're going to have to—to join forces with Old Neap and *make* him see sense, aren't you?"

Aunt stared very hard at Andy, her little wrinkled face all puckered up into a hundred worried lines.

"What you say is sense," she agreed at last. "but what I can do about it, I'm not at all sure. My powers aren't what they were and that's a fact. But I daresay nothing lasts for ever, not even a magic touch. Well, desperate situations call for desperate measures, so I'll try and take a tuck in time. Hold my hands, the pair of you, and Ella, I'll need your help."

Ella and Andy did as they were told and Aunt closed her black eyes and began to whisper under her breath. There was no glowing green light this time; in fact, nothing at all seemed to be happening, except that the sounds of the sea and the wind grew fainter and fainter, until it was so quiet Andy could distinctly hear the thumping of his own heart.

"Everything's stopped!" said Ella.

And it had.

The other four people on the beach had frozen into complete stillness, so that they looked as if they were carved out of rock. The birds, too, were motionless, as were the clouds up above and the sea below. It was as if a film had suddenly become stuck and turned into a photograph.

"I can't hold on for long," Aunt whispered. "Now, will he come or won't he?"

As she spoke, part of the photograph stirred into life and the crest of a big roller, which seconds before had been about to break on the oily beach, opened up and a peevish voice said, "Now what? Who's done this, then? As though I haven't got enough to deal with without added interference. Oh, it's you! I might have known it! Always trouble you were!"

Old Neap wasn't at all what Ella and Andy had imagined he would be like. For one thing he was very small, only about the same size as Aunt, and, for another, his little green face was just as puckered and wrinkled as hers was.

He was wearing a kind of knitted seaweed cap, pulled down low over his emerald eyes, round pebble spectacles, and a disreputable old sweater with a lot of holes in it. He looked tired and cross and altogether in a very bad mood.

"Darned oil," he muttered, hitching his tail onto the edge of the wave and plumping up the spray like a cushion, "got it all over my scales. You've aged, Tress, I'd hardly've known you, or whatever you call yourself now."

"Tress, Mistress Tree, Mrs. Tressida," replied Aunt, "I've had to adapt my name to suit the times. And, come to that, you're a lot older yourself."

"Well, I daresay neither of us will see two thousand again," said Old Neap a shade less disagreeably. "I suppose that girl is your goodness-knows-how-many-times-removed niece. She's got the powers, you mark my words, and if she goes on with her magic learning she'll get stuck here, same as you." He cackled nastily. "And as for him," and Old Neap pointed one gnarled little green finger, "he'll be that so-called 'wounded knight,' I daresay, that's supposed to come and rescue you according to the legend. Trust the mighty Sphinx to get *that* little clause into the treaty, artful as a barrelful of sea-lawyers *he* is! Well, he's not like any knight I've ever seen. Where's his armor or his horse or his lance, tell me that!"

"I haven't got them, but I *did* get Mervyn away," Andy said furiously, "so there!"

"Oh, oh, oh, indeed!" said Old Neap, taking off his spectacles and rubbing them on the sleeve of his terrible sweater, "so the catfish hasn't got your tongue after all. Yes, well, I'll give you that. We *nearly* reclaimed him, mind. It was a close-run thing. Well, time's a-wasting and I've got a lot of work to do with all this mucky oil about. We'd never heard of the stuff in my young days. All this machinery and electric this and that'll be the ruination of magic if we don't look out. Well, what's this meeting all about then?"

Andy looked at Aunt, who nodded slowly and said, "I can't hold time much longer, my flower, speak quickly."

"It's like what you said," Andy began in a gabble, "you and your Sea People have got to fight against the oil. Well, the Land People are in the same boat, if you see what I mean, because the oil kills things on the shore as well as in the sea. So it'd be much more sensible if you both joined together and stopped being enemies, because if you don't, well, it won't be just the oil that'll win, it'll be all the other machines and electricity and atomic power and all . . . all that. And in the end there won't be any magic left, wet or dry."

"Doesn't he run on?" said Old Neap, putting his spectacles back on his nose and then looking over the top of them. "I'm not saying I *agree*, and on the other hand I'm not saying that I *disagree*. What I *will* do is put it on the agenda for the next Great Magical Council Meeting. Furthermore, seeing as how I'm in command of three fifths of the magic creatures in the world, I might, I just might, vote in favor of such a motion. Further than that I won't go at this moment in time. You won't be there, though, will you, Tress?" And he looked at her sharply.

Aunt slowly shook her head.

"Strange," Old Neap said, "there I've kept you prisoner all these years and now you're going to get away from me. The funny thing is, I shall miss you, as there's not many of us old ones left. And as for the new generation, well, there's nothing to them. This wounded knight of yours is still dry behind the ears, but he may improve with time. Speaking of which, it's moving on. 'Bye then, Tress."

" 'Bye, Young Neap."

"Nobody calls me that anymore. Drat this blooming itchy oil. It makes my scales fall out something dreadful."

And with a last irritable wave of a gnarled, small green hand, Old Neap slid back into the wave and, as he disappeared with a flip of his tail, the wave began to move, and as it did so everything else came to life, too, and the clouds started to race across the sky and the big wave broke across the oily beach as the birds resumed their struggle and Mr. Remuson said to Officer Morgan, "We'll have to set up a bird-rescue service down at the Fort. You'll organize that, won't you, Mr. Dunk?"

"I've got more than enough to do."

"Are you all right, Aunt?" Ella asked anxiously, for Mrs. Tressida was looking very pale and tired.

"Yes, I'm just weary, my flower. It did give me a turn seeing Young Neap looking so old. But he's still sharp enough. He saw that I'll never go to another meeting of the Magic People, because, you see, I've used up all the magic in me. I'm not a witch anymore. I'm just a very, very old woman. It does feel strange. . . ."

"There, there," said Mrs. Dunk, hurrying over and taking Mrs. Tressida's elbow. "You shouldn't be standing about in this cold wind. You know, Mr. Dunk and I have been thinking for some time that you should move back to the mainland with us. The island's very bad for rheumatism. I've been getting a twinge or two."

"Myself. I mean, yourself," supplied Andy.

"That's it," agreed Mrs. Dunk, "and we'd go tomorrow if we had the money, but we haven't and that's—"

"Not that at all," said Andy, as the very last piece of the puzzle all fell into place. "Fish, skin, and bones, *that's* what Mistress Tress, I mean, that's what *somebody* hinted to me. There's stacks of money back at the Fort. Well, not stacks, perhaps, but some, and, if you find it, some of it must belong to you. Oh, do come on . . . "

And Andy went thumping across the oily beach as fast as he could, with everybody trailing behind him, the seabirds clasped in their arms.

There must have been some curious magic still hanging around in the Fort for Andy to explain away how he had been exploring all over it and had somehow managed to work out that there was a hollow space behind one of the walls in the kitchen. Mr. Dunk rushed off to get his tools, and for once he really did work hard as he chiseled away until at last the hidden door pivoted open.

"Well, I never did," exclaimed Mr. Dunk, knocking a kitchen chair over in his excitement. "Quiet, Tommy. He's very highly bred, you know. Mind, I've always thought there must be treasures and such hidden away here. But, what with one thing and another, I never had the time to search for it. Although, of course, I daresay most of it will belong to you, Mr. Remuson?"

Mr. Remuson picked up the heavy gold coins that had been nestling in a rotting canvas bag at the very back of the hidden vault, and which had somehow been overlooked by later pirates.

"Oh, I wouldn't say that," Mr. Remuson said slowly. "Of course, the Fort's been in the family for many generations."

He took his pipe out and struck a match and, as the little flame plopped up and down, Andy remembered very clearly where he had seen him before. He was the captain of the pirate ship and he was also the centurion who had come to Andy's rescue long, long ago. Aunt was quite right, time did go around and around in circles.

"Since you and Mrs. Dunk have looked after the Fort for so long," Mr. Remuson went on, sending out a cloud of smoke, "I daresay quite a lot of the reward fund will go to you. Debts must always be paid, and you've done sterling work here."

And if he was looking at Mrs. Dunk, rather than Mr. Dunk, with just a suspicion of a twinkle in his eyes, nobody but Aunt noticed it. Then Mr. Remuson glanced at Andy, and just for a very brief moment Andy, the wounded knight, and someone who could have been in charge of the R.XII, which once led directly to Rome, seemed to be looking at each other across hundreds and hundreds of years. Then Officer Morgan, who had been counting the money, said to no one in particular, "Funny, you know, there used to be an old tale in my family that once upon a time there was a pirate or two among our ancestors!"

"You with a pirate in the family, that's a good one," said Mr. Dunk. "Maybe there was smuggler or two knocking about as well! Hee-haw, hee-haw, hee-haw!"

"Oh, my stars," said Mrs. Dunk, looking quite distracted, "isn't this a treat, then? It means we can go back to the mainland and buy a nice little piece of property with goats and ducks and chickens and there'll be no more trouble with the television and . . ."

"And that reminds me," said Mr. Dunk, settling back in

his chair beside the stove. "It's the big soccer match tonight, but the reception's so bad I don't suppose we'll be
able to see a thing."

"If, no, *when*, we move over to the mainland," said Mrs.
Dunk, plucking at Mrs. Tressida's arm, "we really would
like it very much if you came and made your home with us.
Up till now it's only been a dream of ours, but we do have
this little plot all marked out, and the last list we had from
the agents showed it was still on the market. It's not grand,
mind, but it's woodland and there's a big pond, and a little
village down the lane. It'd be ever so—"

"Homely," agreed Mrs. Tressida, "How very, very kind
of you. I should like it *extremely*, my."

"Flower," said Mrs. Dunk, "well that is nice, then. Oh,
it's a shame about the oil and the birds. Wicked, I call it, all
this oil coming ashore. They should do something about it.
Mr. Dunk was saying only yesterday . . ."

"Well, so that's that," Andy said, when at last Mr. Remuson and Officer Morgan had driven off, taking with them
both the pirate gold and the seabirds who were to be taken
in by the animal shelter.

"Not quite," replied Ella, who having taken Aunt upstairs to have a nap, had returned to the Dunks' kitchen and
was sitting on her heels in front of the stove.

"Yes, it is," said Andy, resting his bad leg on a stool and
scratching it under the plaster with Mrs. Dunk's knitting
needle. "Mervyn's safe back in his right time as a land
person. Aunt's not magic anymore, so she can travel across
water and go and live with the Dunks and not be homesick.
And the Dunks are okay because they'll have enough

money to buy their house. I never realized till we met Old Neap that Aunt was also Tress and Mistress Tree."

"I did. But, Andy, what I was trying to tell—"

"And Mr. Remuson was once a centurion and a pirate captian and Officer Morgan was a pirate too, until he became a smuggler and—"

"Will you *listen*," Ella said in a furious whisper. "It's all right for all of *them*, but what about *me*? If I've got magic powers, and Aunt and Old Neap think I have, then does that mean that *I'm* stuck now?"

The wounded knight stopped scratching and stared at Ella's worried little face. She looked as if she might start crying in a minute.

"Now look here," said Andy very quickly, "we don't know for *sure* that you're a proper witch yet, so don't get in a state about it. Anyway," he took a deep breath, "even if you are, I'll rescue you somehow. Okay?"

"Okay," agreed Ella, starting to cheer up. "What's the matter, Mr. Dunk?"

"Blooming TV," grumbled Mr. Dunk. "I'll bet we won't get the match."

He got up and went over to the set and gave it a thump, which sent Tommy running for his basket. Two seconds later the set came on and both the sound and vision were perfect.

"I always was good with electrical work," said Mr. Dunk, settling himself back in his chair.

"Well, you can't be much of a witch *yet*," Andy said in Ella's ear. Then decided it was high time that he fitted in the very, very last piece of the puzzle, and he thumped over to the telephone and dialed the mainland. In a very short time he heard his mother's voice on the other end. It was as clear as if she had been in the next room.

"Mum," said Andrew Jones, the wounded knight, balancing on his good leg, "I've got an awful lot to tell you. Yes, *of course* I'm all right. Mum, you know how you kept saying it's not everybody who's lucky enough to go and stay on an island? Yes, you did. Well, Mr. and Mrs. Dunk are leaving the Fort and Mr. Remuson, he's the one who owns it, is looking for a new caretaker who'd just cook for a *few* people, and Officer Morgan says he'll do the repair work and . . . What do you mean, sticking my nose into things? Mum, *will you listen!* What I'm saying is, don't you think it would be even more lucky if we actually *lived* on the island?"